THE FOREST OF FAYLEEN

Book One of the Alaina Jackson Trilogy

LORRYN HOLT

ARCHWAY PUBLISHING

Archway Publishing books may be ordered
through booksellers or by contacting:

Archway Publishing
1663 Liberty Drive
Bloomington, IN 47403
www.archwaypublishing.com
1 (888) 242-5904

ISBN: 978-1-4808-6024-7 (sc)
ISBN: 978-1-4808-6025-4 (hc)
ISBN: 978-1-4808-6026-1 (e)

Library of Congress Control Number: 2018904291

Print information available on the last page.

Archway Publishing rev. date: 04/16/2018

DEDICATION

To the men, women, and children affected by 9/11. This story is for you and your courage.

Acknowledgements

MY MOM AND DAD, FOR INSPIRING ME AND PUSH-
ing me to hold the bar high, and don't stop fighting until you
get there. My best friends, my sisters as I call them, Autumn
and Sadie, for sticking with me through thick and thin and
encouraging me to never stop doing what I love. My big
brother Micah, who was my inspiration for Josh - the big,
bad, protective ... teddy bear. Jon Deschenes, my amazing
artist, for working so diligently, being extremely patient with
me, and using his creative brilliance to truly make my story
come to life. My grandparents, both biological and honorary,
for being the John and Liz Williams of my life story. J.R.R.
Tolkien, for inspiring me to create my own worlds and use my
imagination to create people and creatures that only I can.
And God, who never left my side, who guided my fingers to
write and my mind to worlds I could never have imagined on
my own. The Great Storyteller of Creation - His Book inspires
my life.

Contents

PROLOGUE

WIZARD FAYLEEN CRYSTAL PUSHED OPEN A LARGE wooden door, and stepped out taking a deep breath as she looked around at her beautiful castle courtyard. She slowly walked to her garden, with a few attendants following close behind. Fayleen swept up her watering can and drizzled water over her patch of beautiful white Wishing Stars. As she turned to water her many other flowers, she gasped and her hand flew to her heart. She stumbled back into her attendant's arms. Her eyes widened.

"She's awake! She's awake!" the wizard wheezed.

"Who, my lady, who?" one of the attendants asked, supporting her arm.

"Witch Hazel! She's awake!"

The attendants looked to each other in confusion. Finally, one spoke. "My lady, that isn't possible. She can't be awake. She is sealed off in the mountains. Far from here. Guarded with our finest men, and the finest spells. It simply isn't possible."

"Look!" another cried, pointing to the sky. A beautiful red dragon soared above them, but was falling quickly into a landing. As the dragon landed on the Castle grounds, a young man slid off its saddle and ran toward them, holding his arm.

"My lady, I bear horrific news." the young man gasped,

trying to catch his breath. He gripped his torn shirt sleeve as blood trickled through his fingers.

"Out with it, Luke. What has happened?" one of the attendants spoke, her voice shaking.

"My men and I were on patrol in the hills, guarding the sleeping place of Witch Hazel, and we were attacked. Everyone else is gone. And Witch Hazel has escaped."

1

ᑎEW ᑭEOPLE, ᑎEW ᑭLACES

"MISS JACKSON? MISS JACKSON!" THIRTEEN YEAR old Alaina Jackson, better known as Lane, groggily opened her eyes and looked about her. As she brushed her waist-length bleach blond hair out of her face and out of her mouth, she expected to see her hot-pink room, with her mom smiling over her, but what she saw was very different. The inside of an empty plane, a frown of a *very* impatient flight attendant.

Uh-oh. It wasn't a dream, thought Lane frantically. It all came suddenly rushing back. The twin towers collapsing on hundreds of people, including her parents, the judge ordering her to go live with two people she had never even met before ...

"Miss Jackson, we are here in Tennessee now, but unless you want to go all the way to California, I suggest you get out now," the flight attendant said, exasperated.

Lane nodded distantly. She heaved herself up out of the miniature plane seat. She stretched and shook her head as if to shake away the sleepiness.

The flight attendant practically shoved Lane's carry-on into her arms. *She really can't wait to get rid of me. Well, the feeling is mutual.* Lane thought with a smirk. When she stepped out of the plane, she had to throw her hand up in front of her eyes to keep the blinding rays out. She slowly walked into the airport and was relieved to find it not only quite shady but also air-conditioned. She reached into her pocket and pulled out a picture of two very country-looking elderly people. Now to find her grandparents. She looked around, finally locating them. She whispered a short, quiet prayer, then walked over to meet her new guardians.

"E-excuse me ... I'm looking for John and Liz Williams." Lane stumbled over her carefully practiced words. The couple slowly turned around.

"Lane?" whispered the gray-haired woman Lane assumed to be her grandma Liz. Lane suddenly felt like she was coming home. She threw herself in the arms of her grandparents and was relieved to feel their arms wrapping around her. Her grandpa John suddenly picked her up and swung her around, laughing.

"I didn't think it was possible, but you are even prettier

than your picture," he said with a very thick country accent. "Just like your mama." He shook his silver-topped head almost dismissively. "Now," he announced, adjusting the strap on his denim overalls, "let's go get your bags." Seconds later, he was marching off with the others in tow.

Lane stared out the back window of a large Chevy truck, in awe of the beauty around her. She reached in her purse, never looking away from the window, and pulled out her camera. She smiled as she snapped pictures of the hundreds of trees in front of her.

"Grandpa?" She smiled. The word had sounded good to say. "Are there any good places to take pictures around here?" she had asked as they had left the airport.

"Everywhere you look," he said, chuckling.

"My favorite place is in the woods behind the house. So peaceful. You know," he said thoughtfully, "your mama loved it too. When she was a little girl, she would just go. Never told anyone where she was going, never told anyone when she was going. She would be back there for hours." He had smiled at the recollection. Lane grinned at the first of many memories she would share with her grandpa. She leaned back, lost in her thoughts. Then she got curious.

"Grandpa?" she asked.

"Ma'am?"

"How far from here is the house?"

"A long way from here. We won't be getting there tonight. We'll be getting a hotel," he replied.

"How? We are in the middle of nowhere! We past the last hotel miles ago." Lane was confused.

"True. But you will just have to wait and see," Grandpa said with a mysterious glint in his eye.

"**Lane?** Hon, we are almost there. Wake up!" Grandma said gently.

"Huh?" Lane asked groggily, barely awake. She rubbed her eyes and lay her head back on the cool window.

"Stay awake," said Grandpa, chuckling. "We'll be there soon."

Lane glanced out the window and saw a light just ahead of them. "Oh, Grandpa!" Lane gasped as they pulled up to a large lodge.

"Welcome to the best bed-and-breakfast on this side of the world!" Grandpa laughed. He stepped out of the car, walked around to the other side, and then opened his wife's and granddaughter's doors.

"Whoa," breathed Lane. Trees surrounded the area around the huge log building. Lane reached to her purse and pulled out her camera to snap a couple of pictures. Then, she reached out and grabbed her grandfather's hand, as she had done to her father only moments before …

Suddenly Lane was back in New York, in her father's arms. He ran, panting hard, for he had run down four stories, fighting through the people, trying to get his baby girl out of the collapsing building. Suddenly he stopped, turning around. There, his wife knelt by a child who was stuck under a fallen beam, the child's parents lying still nearby. He turned back around, ran through the doors, set her on the concrete, and said hoarsely, "Lane, stay here; I have to go back."

"No! Daddy, please don't leave me!" Lane cried, gripping her father's hand.

"Lane, I have to. I love you," he said emotionally. He turned around, facing the building. He took off in a sprint, bursting through the glass doors and then lifting a beam off a small child. Lane then heard the sickening squeal of an airplane, then the explosion—

"Lane?" Her grandpa knelt before her, bringing her back in the present.

"Lane, honey, are you okay?" her grandma asked, concerned.

"I'm okay," Lane whispered, her voice barely audible. They slowly walked inside.

"**Hello** there! Welcome to the Holtstone B and B!" A friendly and rather elderly man greeted them warmly.

"Hey, Jared," Grandpa replied with a smile.

"Howdy, John," the man Grandpa identified as Jared replied with a grin and a twinkle in his eye. Grandpa walked over to the wooden counter and accepted a key.

"Room five. I will see you in the morning!" Jared proclaimed cheerily.

Lane smiled then trudged up the stairs sleepily. They were greeted by a living room with a fire rolling in the stone fireplace.

"Wow!" Lane whispered.

"How did you—" Grandma started as she touched Grandpa's arm.

He interrupted. "When y'all were asleep, I called ahead to Jared and asked if he could light up a fire and have the room nice and toasty when we got here. It's quite chilly outside." He smiled and took the bags down a short hallway. "Lane!" he called. "Come on down here."

Lane sleepily trudged down the hallway. She stepped in a brightly lit room and was surprised to find it a mix of her favorite colors, with dark-green walls, a brown dresser, and a white bed with a deep-brown comforter.

"Here is your room for tonight. Now, it's pretty late, so why don't you go ahead and get ready for bed?"

Lane nodded, and she opened her suitcase, pulled out her toothbrush and pajamas, and quietly walked to the bathroom.

"Good night, sweetie!" Grandma called as Lane padded back to her room.

"Good night!" Lane replied.

She finished in the bathroom, climbed into her bed, and proceeded to pull up her covers and get comfortable, but she was reluctant to close her eyes.

"**Good** morning!" Lane said groggily as she walked down the stairs to the breakfast nook. Grandpa and the host laughed.

"It certainly is," said Jared as he pulled out a chair for her to sit down next to her grandpa.

"Thank you," she said. She walked over, rubbing her eyes in an attempt to wake up. She sat and lifted her menu. Not ten minutes later, she dove into a hearty breakfast of waffles, bacon, sausage, and a tall glass of milk. Her grandpa laughed. When she slowed down, she glanced over at her grandpa and then sighed. "Grandpa?" she asked.

"That's me," he replied.

"I have a question," she said seriously.

"Well, that's how we get answers."

"Why did my mom like the woods so much? What's back there? Was there a specific place she went? I mean, I am gonna live there; I would like to see what my mom saw. And if I am going to go find it, I probably should know what I'm looking for ... " she hurried through her words nervously.

Her grandpa looked thoughtful, as if he wasn't sure how to answer. "Well, I don't know why she liked the woods so much, though it is hard to not like the woods. I don't know exactly where she went. She never told me specifically. And as for what's back there, I'm not sure," he explained slowly. "But I have a feeling it could be an adventure." And he had a mysterious glint in his eye.

Lane leaped out of the truck, almost before it stopped. She stared in awe at the beautiful home before her that was now hers. A tall log home, wooden shutters, a sturdy oak door, and a beautiful, large green yard with a ... *doghouse?* Lane started to ask where the dog was; then, suddenly, a large chocolate Lab burst out of the doghouse, barking all the way.

"Uh ... Grandpa?" Lane asked uncertainly. "Is he friend— *oof!*" The gigantic Lab bounded up and knocked her over! Lane giggled as he licked her face. "I guess that answers the question." Lane laughed.

Grandma chuckled. "That's Davy. We just got him a few weeks ago. Your grandpa saw an ad in the paper and just had to have him." She rolled her eyes.

Grandpa laughed, then said, "Don't let her fool you, Lane. She loves that dog to death. She feeds the dog better than she feeds me." They laughed lovingly at each other.

Lane smiled, though, almost overcome by the feeling of longing for her parents. "They did that too," she whispered emotionally, tears in her eyes.

"What was that, sweetie?" Grandma smiled at her but was obviously concerned.

"Nothing. I'm fine." Lane forced a fake smile as she pushed her parents' faces into the back of her mind.

2

ROOMS AND RIVERS

LANE LET OUT A LOW WHISTLE WHEN SHE STEPPED in the house. "It's- it's beautiful!" she exclaimed, facing her grandma.

Grandma chuckled. "It's *country*, hon." And indeed it was. The walls a light brown color, a couch and recliner, both a deep hazelnut hue, and a ceiling-high stone fireplace, which was obviously the focus of the room. And above the fire a large wooden mantel hung, covered in pictures. As Lane drew close, she realized that those pictures were of her! Even though she had never met them, and didn't know anything about them, they seemed to know quite a bit about her. Her eyes scanned over them; and then filled with tears as one in particular caught her eye, one of her and her parents in the park back home. Her father had Lane on his shoulders, her mother was laughing at something he had said, and little Lane, only about five years old, was grinning from her perch that had made her feel like a princess. She rubbed her thumb over the picture frame. *You will always be my little princess.* The words that her father had repeated so often rang loud in her ears.

"Honey?" Lane snapped out of her trance at her Grandma's voice.

"Yes, Ma'am?" she called.

"Come up and see your room!"

"Okay!" Lane replied. She gave one last look at the picture, her fingers brushing over her parents faces, then dashed up the stairs.

"Wow!" Lane exclaimed. The room, painted a pale green, seemed to sparkle from the light coming through the full length windows. There was a large oak dresser with a long mirror attached to the top, a full-sized bed with a light brown and pale green quilt on top of a dark brown comforter. A comfy rocking chair sat right next to a lofty book shelf.

"Do you like it?"

"Are you kidding? I love it! How did you know my favorite colors?"

"These are your favorite colors?"

"Yup!"

"Well, what do you know. These used to be your mama's favorite colors too."

"I didn't know that."

"They were."

An awkward silence was created, both thinking deeply about Lane's mom.

"Well, um, I'll let you get settled." Grandma's voice broke the silence.

Lane nodded. Grandma patted the luggage awkwardly, then left the room. Lane slowly walked over to the full bookshelf and was surprised to see the books were only about nature, flowers, and trees. *Grandpa wasn't kidding when he said she loved the woods.* She smiled, running her hand over the rows of books. She found one book that had no title at all. Curious, she pulled it out, coughing from its dust. She made a face, then brushed off as much as she could. She opened it and quietly read the messy handwritten note on the first page.

"The Woodland Diary of Izabella Williams?" she mumbled. *Mom?*

Lane slowly flipped through the book, confused. Her grandpa hadn't mentioned her mother's love of the woods went *this* far. She had written down page after page of research involving trees, edible plants, poisonous plants, herbs, natural medicines, and more. Lane felt overwhelmed by the knowledge in this book. Even more so that it was her mother who wrote it. She noticed that every page had a date on it. The dates went from 1968, when she was a teen, all the way to 1987, the very year she got married and left this place. *Why did you stop? What happened, Mom?*

"Lane! Can you come down, please?" Grandpa called.

"Yeah!" Lane yelled back, tossing the book on her bed.

"I was going to go take a walk down to the river. Want to join me?" Grandpa asked, with a twinkle in his eye.

"Yeah! I really want to see the area. Let me go grab my jacket and camera. I want to get some pictures." Lane sprinted up the stairs. Grandpa winked at Grandma.

"She is just like our Izabella." Grandpa mused. Grandma started to say something, then Lane came running down the stairs, and she stopped abruptly.

"I'm ready." Lane said, a little breathless.

"Then let's go." Grandpa replied. Grandma watched as the two of them walked down the gravel driveway.

She looked up, and said with tears in her eyes, "She's just like you, Iz. Just like you."

"Grandpa?" Lane broke the silence as they crunched through the gravel.

"Yes?" Grandpa asked.

Lane sighed, waited a moment, then asked "You got my mom her diary, didn't you?" Her grandpa stopped in his tracks.

"You found it," he whispered.

"Yeah. What is it? Why did she write all of that down? *How* did she write all of that down?" Lane hurried through her words. Her grandpa was still silent. *Why did I bring it up?* Lane thought.

Grandpa continued along the road, then said, "Lane, your mama loved the woods. I told you that much." Lane nodded, and he continued. "She knew a lot, and she did everything she could to get more and more information. She wanted to write a real book one day. She knew all the plants; she knew all the trees, the flowers … But, you know, I never did figure out why she stopped. Maybe you will," he said thoughtfully.

Lane started to ask him another question, but then he exclaimed, "Here we are! Welcome to the Laurel River." He grinned. Lane quickly pulled out her camera and snapped a couple pictures of the rapidly flowing river.

"What on earth happened to you two?" Grandma exclaimed as two dripping-wet, shivering people came walking in through the door.

"I asked if I could roll up my pants and wade, and he said 'Sure', but he opted out. He *said* he was just going to sit on the bank." Lane said pointedly, rolling her eyes at her Grandpa while her teeth chattered. When he tried to defend himself, Grandma held up a hand.

"Wait a minute! She's the one telling the story. Go ahead, Lane."

"Ok, well," she continued, rubbing her arms to warm them, "He splashed water on me and got my shirt soaking wet. So I did the same thing to him," she said innocently.

"Is that the whole story?" Grandma said with fake sternness. On the inside, she was already quaking with laughter. Grandpa, on the other hand, was not trying to conceal it. He leaned against the door and was trying to breathe through gasps of laughter. Lane snorted.

"Not exactly," she continued, "We both kept on splashing each other; then he stepped into the water, and the splashes starting getting bigger! Then," she said, at this point, she herself was speaking through fits of giggles, "I took a step backwards, and I slipped, and I-"

"GRABBED MY HAND!" Grandpa howled through laughter.

"Well, then we BOTH went down, and after tumbling a few feet down the river, here we are." Lane laughed. At this point, Grandma simply could not hold it in. They all leaned against each other and laughed, forgetting all the worries, fears, and sadness that they had fought so hard to get rid of before.

"You both are acting like little kids!" Grandma scolded.

"Oh, you say that now," Grandpa attempted to speak, "But you know you would have been right there with us!" And that, of course, triggered another fit of laughter.

About half an hour later Lane walked down stairs in some warm, dry clothes very thankful for hot showers.

"Lane! Honey, is that you?" Grandma called from the kitchen.

"Yup!" Lane called back, walking toward the direction of the kitchen. She walked in and saw her grandma standing by the counter, whipping up something that looked an awful lot like ...

"Chocolate chip cookies!" Lane exclaimed, surprised. Her grandma screamed and threw the spatula across the room, barely missing Lane's head. Grandma grabbed her heart, gasping.

"You scared the living daylights out of me!" she scolded. Lane put on a fake scared look. Her grandma sighed, then answered the beginning question. "Yes, they are chocolate chip cookies. Supper is almost ready," Grandma waved her hand to the other side of the room where a large pot of soup sat on an old stove. Lane walked over and lifted the lid, smelling the bubbling pot of-

"Sausage and potato soup." Grandma smiled as she watched her. "And, I thought after that dunk you took," she snickered a little before continuing, "you and your Grandpa could use some warm chocolate chip cookies." She finished with an innocent smile.

"You just wanted something with chocolate, didn't you?" Lane teased. Like every other girl.

"Yup," Grandma admitted with a grin.

The moan of the falling building, the screams, the sound of people yelling, beating on the glass, trying to get out …

Lane panted as she sat bolt upright in bed, soaked in sweat.

"Why can't the nightmares just *GO AWAY*!" Lane whispered, tears filling her eyes.

She looked at her clock.

3:39.

Lane pulled up the covers, and clenched her pillow against her face trying to block out the haunting screams.

———◦◦◦———

The next morning, Grandma poked her head in through the door and smiled at a snoring Lane. "Lane," she said, turning on the light. Lane stirred, then stilled again. "Lane!" Grandma walked over and shook her arm. "Wake up!" she said gently. Lane sat up, rubbing her eyes.

"What time is it?" Lane asked sleepily.

"Eight o'clock." Grandma replied. Lane flopped back down on the bed. "If you don't get up, I'm going to go get Grandpa. And his methods of waking someone up involve a bucket of cold water, but if that's what you want ... " Grandma started toward the door-

"Wait!" Lane leaped out of bed. "I'm awake! NO COLD WATER!" she exclaimed.

Grandma laughed. "Come on, sleepyhead. Breakfast is ready." Grandma said. Lane got up, rubbed her eyes again, and walked over to the dresser.

"What should I wear for the woods?" she mumbled.

Lane walked down the stairs to the table catching a delicious smell on the way. Something smells good.

"Morning!" Grandpa greeted her.

"Morning, Grandpa," Lane replied, sliding into her seat. Grandma walked in with a bowl of gravy in one hand, and a plate of biscuits in the other. She set them down carefully, then back in the kitchen she went.

"Does she live in there or something?" Lane asked.

"Can't complain none." He patted his bulging stomach. Out scurried Grandma again with a plate of bacon and a large bowl of scrambled eggs.

"Can't say that I would either!" Lane replied.

"What are you two scheming?" Grandma asked suspiciously as she sat down with them.

Grandpa and Lane glanced at each other and then looked back at Grandma. "Why nothing! How could you ever suspect us of any wrong?" Grandpa asked.

"Oh, I have no idea! I can just see your halos glowing," Grandma retorted.

3

TREES AND TROUBLES

"GRANDPA!" LANE CALLED FROM THE DOOR.

"Yeah!" came a response from the living room.

"I'm going to go walk in the woods, ok?" she yelled.

"Ok! Be careful!"

Lane grinned and took off out the door. She ran about fifty feet and then stared at the beautiful woods before her.

Woods doesn't quite describe it. Forest is a better word. She smiled and stepped in, pulling out her camera. After walking only ten yards, she realized why her mother loved it so much. The trees themselves were incredible. Oaks, pines, cedars, poplars, and the list continued. They went from one hundred foot poplars, to five foot saplings. She grinned and started running, stopping to snap pictures along the way. She slowed and doubled over, out of breath. Looking up, Lane found herself facing two tall trees ... *intertwined?* Two tall, yet slanted trees stood about four feet apart, their branches straining to reach for each other. As Lane's gaze travelled up the tree trunks, she saw that they met about six feet up from the ground, and circled around each other, never parting again. They seemed to grow together from that place up. It almost looked like a doorway. Lane pulled her mother's diary out of her jacket pocket and quickly flipped to the tree section, attempting to find what it was. Lane stopped at one description that matched it down to the last detail. Lane looked at the name. "Huh? Unknown?" she whispered to herself. Lane pulled her camera out and snapped a couple pictures of it. Perhaps Grandpa would know what it was. Though she had a sneaking suspicion he wouldn't.

She stared at the tree and thought she saw a small glimmer near the roots. But as soon as she looked toward it, it was gone. Lane furrowed her brow and stepped forward to take a closer look. Just a little closer and she could touch it, just a little- AHH! Lane screamed as she tripped on a root and went flying ... right through the opening. Lane felt like she was rolling downward, though she knew the forest was flat, then-OUCH! Everything faded to black.

Lane tried to open her eyes, but- OW! Her head hurt, and a small pressure was applied to her chest. Her eyes fluttered then opened slightly. She then realized that, standing *on her chest,* were three little people. They were not even a foot tall, and looked something like ... well, fairies. Lane laughed at herself. *Fairies? Ok, I'm just dreaming.*

Then one of the miniscule creatures tilted her head making her long, curly, red hair tumble down past her shoulders to her waist. She grinned and said in a tiny voice, "Hello!"

Lane promptly passed out again.

When she woke up, she found herself being shaken by one of two short, hefty men. Lane looked closely. They looked identical, only four feet tall at most, with their long, dark beards coming to their waist, and black hair falling to thickly muscled shoulders. *Dwarves?* Lane opened her mouth to scream. The dwarf quickly covered her mouth with one of his rough hands, and signaled to be quiet with the other. Lane nodded, terrified.

"Ok," he said in a surprisingly deep, gruff voice. "I'm going to remove my hand, and you are going to stay quiet. Got it?"

Lane nodded.

The man removed his hand. Lane stared in shock. The three, tiny "fairies" giggled and pointed to her as they whispered amongst themselves.

"Ok, let me get this straight." Lane said, frustrated after they made a bad attempt to explain where she was. "You two are dwarves." They nodded. "You guys are fairies." The trio grinned like they just won the lottery. "And *I* am the weird one here?" Lane exclaimed.

"Yup!" piped up the red-haired fairy. "You look funny."

Lane would have giggled at her cuteness, but she was too confused. "What? Where am I?"

"Evoron Hills," one of the dwarves said matter-of-factly.

"And where is that?"

"Well, it's here," said one of the fairies, as if that made perfect sense.

"Ok, we are clearly not getting anywhere with location," Lane said. "So, let's try this. *Who* are you?"

"Oh, that's simple," a blue-shirted dwarf answered. "I am John, and this is my twin Jack." The other dwarf in a bright red shirt waved hi.

Lane nodded to acknowledge him, and then the red-haired delicate fairy spoke up.

"I am Rose, but you can call me Rosie." Lane took a moment to study each of them. The pale-skinned Rosie wore a rose petal dress, had bright red curly hair, and delicate pale yellow wings adorned her back.

"I am July, but you can call me Jules," another continued, this one tanned, wearing a short, bright yellow, jonquil-petal dress, golden hair with sun-bleached streaks, and cloud white wings that fluttered behind her. She looked like the persona of summer.

"And I am Oakley, and you can call me Oakley," another laughed, this one's flesh, a deep brown. He wore a shirt of sewn oak leaves, with light brown wings protruding, the dark brown design on them looking like the grain of a wooden board. He had on little brown breeches made of a stiff fabric, and an acorn top hat, which was sliding off sideways from the top of his shaggy mop of brown hair. He giggled as he pushed it back up into it's position. From the looks of it, it wasn't bound to stay sitting there for very long.

"And I want to know what is going on here!" They all whipped around at the new voice. A very tall boy stood behind them with his bow drawn, two girls on one side, one with another bow, and one with daggers. Another boy, a mere preteen, stood on his other side armed with two silver swords that looked far too big for him. All were in an offensive stance.

"Willow! Lea!" The two fairies who had introduced themselves as Rosie and Jules flew forward into the two girls' arms. The girls slid their weapons back in their sheathes, and then hugged the fairies tightly. Oakley saluted the boys, and the youngest cracked a smile. As he put his swords in a double sheath on his back, he swung Oakley up to sit on his shoulder. The last boy, obviously the leader, did not move, his arrow trained on Lane.

"Josh! Put your bow down, for Fayleen's sake!" the oldest girl said. The boy, identified as Josh, slowly lowered his bow and smoothly removed the arrow, placing it in the quiver attached to his back. He swung the bow over his head and under one of his arms. He spoke with authority, "Who are you? Where do you come from?"

Lane's voice shook from intimidation. "My name is Lane. I am from New York-uh- Tennessee." Her courage shot up. "Who are you?"

Josh's eyes remained cool at her sudden outburst. "I am Josh. This is Willow." The girl who told him to put his bow down waved slightly and gave her a motherly smile. "This is Lea." The young girl smiled warmly at Lane. "And this young boy is Quinn." He grinned at her with admiration. Probably because she stood up to Josh. Obviously not many people did. Lane had a sneaking suspicion she would wind up paying for it later.

"Why are you here?" asked Josh sternly.

"Well, if I knew where 'here' was, I could tell you," Lane replied promptly.

Josh looked confused. "You are in Evoron Hills. Right over there," he pointed to a large tree-line, "is The Forest of Fayleen."

"How are you here, if you don't even know where here is?" asked Willow kindly.

"Well, I tripped and fell between two trees, and I got knocked out. Then when I woke up, they were here." Lane explained, pointed to the fairies and dwarves. Josh turned to them.

"How did she get here?" he asked, ignoring her.

"Well," Jules started, embarrassed. "We went up to the highest of Evoron Hills, just for fun, and then we saw the portal. Of course, we knew what it was, and why it must have appeared, so Oakley walked over to the portal and looked in. He thought he saw somebody, and then he thought she saw him, so he hid."

"But she came closer," Oakley continued, "and then she fell through the portal-"

Lane interrupted. "Why do you keep calling it a portal?"

"Supposedly, it's a portal to another world. But it's just an old myth. It should only appear when a new wizard is near. Then it will disappear until some courageous act has been done," Lea explained.

"But it's true," Rosie insisted.

"Whatever you say, Rosie," Willow said comfortingly, winking at Lane.

"Please continue, Jules," Josh pleaded impatiently, rolling his eyes at the old story.

"Ok, well, she fell through, and started rolling down the hill. We chased after her, but when we found her, she was knocked out. Hit her head on a rock. Jack and John went to find the tree again while we watched her, but they couldn't find it."

"How do you explain that, Lea?" Rosie shot.

"Wait," Lane interrupted again, "what do you mean they couldn't find it again? They have to! I have to get back home."

"Look, there is only one thing to do. You will come to Crystal Castle with us, and we will see what Fayleen wants us to do. Maybe there is some way we can make it reappear, or send you back, or something," Josh said, and that was the final word.

Lane gasped for breath. They had been walking for *hours*; and the heavy backpacks, filled with who-knows-what, weren't helping anything.

"Let's stop for the night," Josh called back to the rest of the group as he walked over to a small river.

Everyone sighed with relief as they dropped their heavy leather packs. Willow walked back about twenty yards into the woods and started putting together a campsite. Lea busied herself digging through the packs to find something to cook for supper for everyone, and quickly sent Quinn, Jack, and John on their way to find some firewood. The fairies flited from here to there always moving around. It was impossible to tell what they were doing. Josh trudged over to a large flat rock next to the river, set down his pack, and then plopped himself next to it. He stared at the drooping sun and the thousands of different colors it cast about the sky. Lane glanced over and saw his head drop a little and then jerk up, trying to push the sleepiness away. Apparently, Lane wasn't the only one who noticed.

Willow walked over placing a gentle hand on his shoulder. He glanced up.

Willow spoke in a soft tone; though Lane couldn't hear what was said, she grinned as Josh nodded, got up, walked over to the campsite, and laid out a blanket. Lane snorted a little as he lay down and almost instantly started snoring.

Willow must have a lot of say around here. She's like a mother hen. Lane thought, smiling. Lea looked at her strangely.

"What's so funny?" she asked.

"Nothing," Lane said, hiding a grin. She looked at the river. "Um, I think I'm going to go wade around a little bit. Is that okay?" Lane asked.

"Sure. I'll call you when supper is ready," Lea replied, going back to digging through the backpacks.

"Ok, thanks," Lane replied.

She walked over to the river, admiring the sparkle of the sun on the water. She pulled off her sneakers, yanked off her socks, and rolled up her pant legs. Lane stepped into the cool water. It felt so good she almost leaped in all together. Then a large group of tiny fish about 5 inches long each swam over to her. Lane stood frozen, not wanting to scare them off. *They are beautiful!* Their bright silver scales were so shiny and reflective they could blind you if you stared too hard.

They horded around her. She smiled at them, and they almost seemed to smile back as they floated listlessly. She dipped her hands in to get a drink from the appealing water. She scooped up a handful of water and raised it a couple inches off the water ... She leaned down just a little further-

"Uh, Lane! I wouldn't do-" But Willow was too late in warning. One of the fish leaped out of the water, only about an inch from her face, whipped around, and slapped her with its tail!

"Augh!" Lane yelled, it's tail sliced into her cheek, not deep, but extremely painful. Then, about twenty others did the same thing. Every time one fish flopped back into the water, another would leap to take its place. They didn't cut her like the first one did, but the sharp slaps were still quite painful. Lane suddenly felt dizzy. Her vision began to swim when she was grabbed and ripped out of the water. She landed with a thud on the river sand. Looking back at the river, her vision slightly came into focus and she watched as Josh ran out of the water while ducking to avoid the flying fish. He jumped out and landed only about a foot from her. He looked over, his eyes widening at the cut.

"Lea! Get me some plantain. Now."

In a few minutes, Lane was laying on a blanket, the cool plant pressed against her cheek. "Why are you guys freaking out?" she asked. "It's only a little cut." Josh and Willow exchanged a look.

Willow sighed. "Those things are more dangerous than meets the eye. They are extremely protective of the waters they inhabit. If you try to drink from it, or swim, they will jump up and smack you. Their tails have small needle-like spines on the top and bottom. Those are filled with poison.

They make you dizzy, delusional; and if there are a lot of cuts, it can kill you. You got lucky with only one, but we still need to take precautions. Plantain is what we call a poison puller. It pulls out infections, poisons; it can even pull out pain, especially in bee stings and such. You should feel better in a few minutes. It's true, the fish are very pretty and very small; but don't underestimate their power because of their size. Even the smallest things can be the most dangerous things in the world." Willow looked solemn.

"What she says is correct." They whirled toward the water.

A mermaid rose out of the water facing them. Lane wasn't sure why she was surprised to see a mermaid too. After all, she was traveling with two hefty dwarves, three crazy fairies, and four warrior elves. Why not add a mermaid to the bunch?

"What the elf says is right," the mermaid continued, "My silverfins are protective of water. But they are more protective of me. When the water leaves, or I leave the water, it weakens me. So they protect me. But, just drinking the water should not be harmful. Here." The mermaid tossed onto the bank a small drawstring bag made of seaweed. Lane gingerly opened it. She gasped. Light poured from the bag's opening. Inside were three pearls, each filled with light.

The mermaid smiled at their shock. "If you need a drink from my river, throw a pearl in the water. It will tell the fish that you are friend and not foe. They will not attack. Do not worry about running out of pearls. The bag is magic. Every time you throw in a pearl, it will reappear in your bag."

The mermaid began to sink underneath the crystal-clear water.

"Wait!" Lane called, getting up and running to the edge. The mermaid turned back around and looked at her. "Why are you helping us? You don't even know who we are," Lane pressed.

The mermaid smiled. "I don't need to. I can tell you are a good person."

"How?"

"You smiled."

"What?"

"You smiled at the fish. Most people would shoo them away without acknowledging them. You smiled," the mermaid said, turning to dive in the water.

"Wait!" Lane cried, not ready to say goodbye. She felt a strong connection to her, even though she wasn't sure why. "What is your name? Will I see you again?"

"So many questions," the mermaid laughed. "But, the answers are, yes. You will see me again. If you are lonely, or need help, just speak to the river. I will hear you. My name is Coral." And with those words she dove into the water and disappeared.

4

Walking to Meet a Wizard

LANE STARED AFTER HER, THEN TURNED TO FIND
everyone gaping at her. "What?"

"That was Coral, Queen of The Rivers, appointed by
Wizard Fayleen herself when The Forest was first created. No
one has seen Coral in centuries. Many said she was dead. But
it was foretold that she would reappear only when we needed
her the most. When The Forest was in danger of destruction,"
Willow said, her voice quivering. She glanced over at Josh to
see his reaction.

"We have to get Lane to the castle. Now," he said grimly. Willow nodded, unable to answer. Even dwarves were silent, and the fairies were mute. Josh cleared his throat, as if trying to clear the air. Willow seemed to snap out of a trance.

"Right, then." She breathed in deeply, then continued, "Jack, John, get more wood for a fire. Rosie, Jules, Oakley, try to find some berries, edible mushrooms, or plants. Just don't go too far. Lea, you can help me get supper ready."

"What can I do?" piped up Quinn.

Willow smiled at him. "You can help Jack and John," she replied. She looked at Lane, "You, on the other hand, are going to lay down."

Lane started to protest, but Josh leaned over and whispered, "Don't even try. I've been trying for a long time. Never seemed to do much good, obviously." Lane bit her lip, trying not to smile.

Maybe he isn't such a grumpy bear after all. Well, maybe a teddy bear.

Willow looked over, curious. "What's so funny?"

"Nothing," Lane suppressed a grin.

Later that evening, Lane lifted her wooden spoon to her lips and back down to her bowl. She stared into the thick stew, then looked around at the circle of people. Everyone ate in an uncomfortable silence. Finally, Lane couldn't stand it anymore. She cleared her throat loudly. Everyone looked up.

"I have an idea."

"What's that?" asked Oakley.

"Let's play a game."

"But we are eating. How can we play a game?" asked Lea.

"We don't have to get up. We can do it right here. Sitting down."

"What kind of game?" asked Willow, intrigued.

"It's called the Thankful Game."

"How do you play?"

"Well, we are supposed to be in a circle, but we have already done that. So, the next step is we go around the circle, and everyone says something they are thankful for."

"Ok. Let's try it!" piped up Jules.

"Ok, well, I'll go first. I'm thankful that I found the tree, and hopefully, some new friends." Lea and Willow smiled at her.

"Can I go now?" asked Rosie, who was sitting to Lane's left.

"Sure."

"I'm thankful that I got to see Lea and Quinn today. I haven't seen them since they came to my village."

Lea was next, and she leaned back and thought for a moment.

"Well, um, I'm glad that I got to come on this trip with Willow. It's been a lot of fun, and I have learned a lot from her and Josh."

Then it was Willow's turn. "I am glad I have such great friends and students. Wow, that makes me sound old. I'm only 19!" Everyone laughed.

One by one, they all went around the circle. Everyone liked the game so much, they decided to play several rounds. Everyone laughed, forgetting all their worries and all their fears. Finally, since everyone was laughing so hard they couldn't breathe, they decided to call it a night.

Willow laid out a blanket for Lane. "I'm sorry I can't do more to make you comfortable. After all, this is your first night here. I wish I could snap my fingers and take you instantly to the Crystal Castle, but unfortunately, I don't have that power. It is pretty rare."

"How does someone get magical power? I mean, how did Witch Hazel get it?"

Willow looked up, surprised.

"Lea told me a little about Wizard Fayleen, Witch Hazel, and what is going on."

"Well, that's fine. It's no big secret. And to answer your question, it is mostly passed down through elven families. But, though it is extremely rare, sometimes it can come randomly to an elf."

Lane nodded deep in thought.

Willow looked around, and noticed everyone else was already in their make-shift beds, the fairies already sound asleep.

"Well, I better get to bed," Willow whispered.

Lane nodded, smiling. Lane laid out on her own bed and pulled the woolen blanket up to her chin, but she wasn't as quick to close her eyes.

———◆———

Smoke ... fire ... the sound of an explosion ... the screams. Lane jerked out of her nightmare and sat up, soaked in sweat. She looked around and saw that everyone else was still fast asleep. She slowly slipped out of her coarse makeshift sleeping bag, shivering from the cool air. She snuck away from the small campsite, deciding that maybe a walk would clear her head. More importantly, she wanted to get rid of the nightmares, even if it was just for a short while. *If only walking away from the nightmares was as easy as walking away from the campsite.*

Due to the sky slowly turning from black to an assortment of deep blues, and pale pinks and oranges, she noticed more and more river sand being mixed with the moist soil. Presently, she found herself back at the small clearing by the river. She smiled at the sound of gurgling water. She found the flat rock and lay down staring at the stars that remained in the slowly transitioning sky.

"Beautiful, isn't it?"

Lane jumped up from her perch on the stone, her heart racing. The corner of Josh's mouth lifted into a half-smile as he morphed out of the edge of the woods. He waved for her to sit back down, then he too sat down and just stared into space. Lane waited for him to speak, but she just couldn't stand the awkward silence any more.

"Why did you follow me?" she burst out.

"Who says I did? I just took a walk." Josh feigned innocence for a moment, but at her hard look, he cracked. "I heard you leave," he admitted. "Are you alright?"

"I just needed to take a walk. Clear my head. It's not every day a girl arrives in a new world. It can be rather stressful, if you haven't picked up on that yet."

"Lane, that's exactly my point. This is a new world. It's not safe for you to just walk off."

She pushed herself off the rock and stood, crossing her arms. "Look I know I'm a girl, but I can take care of myself."

He shook his head, and said, "I never said you couldn't. But you have no idea what is out there. We have things here that would make your worst nightmares cower." At the mention of nightmares, Lane tensed up before sitting back down beside him. Josh looked at her curiously.

"Why did you really leave?" he questioned.

"I needed a walk," she said, feeling guilty about lying.

"Lane-" Josh stopped. He sighed. "Well, this has been a wonderful conversation and all, but we should get back." He glanced up at the quickly rising sun. Lane just nodded. He stood up and stuck out his hand to help her. She pushed his hand away and launched herself from the rock. *I don't need his help with everything. I can take care of myself.* They walked away from the water and into The Forest in complete silence. They finally arrived back at the campsite just as everyone was starting to stir.

"Lane." Josh grabbed her arm, pulling her back toward him. She looked up, questioning. "Just to let you know, you are a terrible liar." She started to reply, but he just smirked and walked off.

"So ... " Lane was ready to talk. They had been walking all day, mostly in complete silence. She looked over at Lea who was walking beside her. "Where are we going again?" she asked.

"To the castle. The one place we will be safe," Lea replied, nervously looking around as if she expected something to leap out of the trees any second.

Lane looked around. Everything was so beautiful here. Why was everyone so skittish? "Why is everyone so scared of such a beautiful forest? What are you afraid of?" she questioned. She didn't want to push, but she needed to know.

Lea gazed into The Forest for a moment, then replied slowly, "Looks can be deceiving. It *is* a beautiful place, and I love The Forest with all my heart. There are many beautiful creatures, plants, people, but there are dangerous ones too. Everything of beauty has an opposite."

"Example, please?" Lane pressed.

"Well, even some flowers are dangerous. Hallu-Flower Pass, a place very close to where we found you, has gorgeous flowers lining the long narrow valley. They are orange, red, even hot pink ... absolutely beautiful. But they emit a poisonous gas, that causes deadly hallucinations. They can drive a person to madness. That is only one out of many poisonous plants. Then you have animals. For instance, Black Dragon Hills, no one has every returned from. Some dragons are good, don't get me wrong. Some we ride, some help carry loads from place to place, some smaller dragons even have magical powers! But dragons, as big and mighty as they may be, can be easily manipulated. Trying to help them, trying to protect The Forest, the people; well, it has really worn her down. Fayleen is trying to find someone to pass it to. To train to be the new wizard."

Lane started to respond, but-

"We're here!" Josh called back.

Having fallen behind, they hurried forward to catch up. Lane looked up and saw a huge, towering, stone castle, ivy strewn across its walls. They walked up to a large, cast-iron gate.

"Who goes there?" yelled down a voice from the top of the wall.

"Luke, it's me!" Josh called.

"Who are those people with you?"

"They are here to see Fayleen."

"She can't see anyone. You know that."

"Luke ... " Josh lowered his voice, and continued, "the Tree appeared."

The young man Josh addressed as Luke walked them swiftly down a long corridor to a tall, thick wooden door. He put his shoulder up against it and with one big shove, the door creaked open. He stepped aside and waved his hand to motion them inside. There, several young women, also elves, quietly bustled around a large silver bed. An elderly woman leaned against a few pillows, her white hair lay in waves falling over her shoulders. A hairpiece circled her head, adorned with white gold flowers, crystals, and delicate silver leaves. It looked like the most beautiful flower vine made from tiny metal thread. The woman wore a pale blue gown, simple medieval style, with flowing sleeves and white lace overlay. Josh hurried over to the side of the bed kneeling beside her. He whispered then looked up for what seemed to be assurance. She nodded slowly, looked up, and smiled at Lane. She spoke, surprising Lane with a light, clear voice. "Excuse us, ladies. I would like to speak with these people alone, please."

Lane was surprised. *She speaks more like one of them than a queen or wizard.* The thought stumped her. *Well, two days ago, I didn't know wizards existed. I honestly don't know how they are supposed to speak.* Her attendants hurried out of the room.

Josh stood up, walked over to Lane, and whispered in her ear, "Go over to her. She wants to speak to you."

Lane slowly walked over keeping her eyes on the floor. She stopped beside the bed and slowly met her calm, blue eyes.

"What is your name, child?" the woman asked softly.

"Um ... Lane. Well, actually, it's Alaina Noel Jackson. But everyone calls me Lane." Lane stammered.

Shock fleeted across her face, but it left as quickly as it came.

"It's alright, child," she continued gently. "I know all this is new to you, and you don't know about our world, but that's just fine."

Lane must have looked confused, because the older woman looked sympathetic. "I apologize, I must start at the beginning." She looked past Lane at Josh and motioned for them to leave. He nodded and ushered everyone out.

Then, she spoke, "My name is Fayleen Crystal. I am a wizard. With the help of my father, King Neilan, and mother, Queen Juniper, we created The Forest. But my father used so much magic that it drained his life's power. On his deathbed he passed The Forest on to me. To protect, to maintain, to be its caretaker. I was honored. I adored The Forest. So I accepted. After he passed my mother helped me fill it with plants, insects, and animals. It was wonderful to spend time with her. She asked me to make the same promise to protect them as well as The Forest. Not long after, we lost her as well. My sister, Hazel, now known as Witch Hazel Black, was furious. She thought that she could care for them just as well as I could. She decided to make her own spells and creatures, her own flowers and plants. She succeeded, but only slightly. She overlooked the small details and put her malice and jealousy into her spells and creatures, while my mother and I put love and care. Many of her spells were defective, and some were just uncontrollable."

"Lea mentioned a place called Hallu-Flower pass. Was that one of the defective spells?" Lane interrupted.

Fayleen sighed, then replied, "Yes. Hallu-flowers are flowers that emit a powerful gas when stirred. Whether it is only by wind, or someone touching them, they are activated. But, there is always a powerful wind blowing through. Another spell. May I continue the story?" Lane blushed and nodded. "Well, as I said, Hazel was furious. She unleased her creatures upon The Forest, death and destruction falling wherever she stepped." A lone tear slipped down the old wizard's face. She sniffled, then continued. "That was my baby sister. The young girl I ran through flower gardens with had turned into a monster. But I knew that somewhere inside she still had good in her. I confronted her and pleaded with her to stop this madness. When she refused, we were plunged into a battle, spell on spell, sister against sister." She sobbed quietly, and Lane could almost feel her pain. She didn't want to press, but she wanted to know more. She started to ask her to continue, but Fayleen spoke. "I caught her off guard, sending a sleep spell her way. I knew it would be harmless to her, and it would keep her from doing any more harm to The Forest. I had vowed to protect it, and protect it I would. Once she was asleep I placed her in the Mist Mountains with spell traps to keep everyone out. But caring for The Forest for so many years has weakened me; and until I have someone to pass my power to, my spells have weakened too. I had a spell to protect The Forest from the evil creatures that try to get in and do harm to my subjects. It has been failing, and more and more monsters have been entering, slaughtering innocents. Another major spell that has weakened was-"

"The Sleep Spell." Lane said, horrified.

"Yes. My sister has awoken."

5

TRAINING AND TRIALS

"OKAY, NOW WHAT ARE WE DOING EXACTLY?" Lane asked, her helmet sliding down her head. She shoved it back and blew a small strand of light blond hair out of her face.

"Hmm. A little big." Willow mumbled to herself as she turned around to face the wall that was covered top to bottom with leather armor. She snatched a different helmet, jerked the first one off Lane's head, and plopped the new one down. She stepped back to examine it. Nodding her head, she said, "Yes, I think that will do." She pulled it off, and placed in into a box with 'ALAINA' written on the front, as she had already done with elbow guards, leg guards, a silver handled dagger, and a few more items.

"Uh-huh. Whatever. Now, *why are we doing this?*"

"Oh, sorry. Sometimes I kind-of zone out." Willow looked back to the armor, obviously avoiding the question.

Lane sighed. "You still didn't answer my question."

"Well … you are going to train."

"For what?"

"You need to know how to protect yourself. Witch Hazel is coming. If she knows you are here it will just make matters worse."

"Why? I'm just a kid. What can I do against a witch?"

"Well, right now, nothing. That's why we are training you. You have to know how to protect yourself, especially from Witch Hazel." She mumbled the name and her eyes darted around the room like the witch might hear her and pounce at any given second.

"It's not like I am going to face her." Lane gave a weak chuckle. Willow seemed very interested in the armor. "Uh, Willow? I'm not going to face her … right?"

Willow knelt by her left side and gestured for Lane to stick her arms out to the sides. As Lane obliged, Willow gave a pull and tightened a strap on Lane's leather chest plate. She waited a moment, then answered. "I can't say for sure. I hope not, but it isn't for me to decide. If it was up to me, I would already be taking you back to find the tree. I would never put you in any danger. You deserve a bright future. One that has nothing to do with this place. It might seem like a fun, beautiful, magical forest, and don't get me wrong, it is; but it is also very dangerous. That's why all elves around here are trained when they are young."

"Like Lea and Quinn?"

"Yeah. They were just supposed to just be on a field trip with us. Josh and I were to judge if they were ready for the final course. We weren't expecting to find anything. We certainly never expected anything like this to happen." Willow stopped. She shook her head, and then tightly fastened a strap with a silver buckle on the top of Lane knee-high leather boots. "Well, what do you think?" Willow asked, trying to lighten the mood.

Lane looked down at herself. The front of her long, nearly white, blond hair was twisted around her head in a crown-like fashion, both sides connecting in the middle, then down her back in a tight braid. She wore an elbow-length green tunic, brown leggings with knee high leather boots. Her fingerless, brown leather gloves matched her backpack, and the wide belt around her waist. Apparently, green and leather was common fashion around here. "I look like you," she grinned.

"If you had dark brown hair, pointed ears, and green eyes, you would blend right in with the elves of The Forest. Those are our racial traits." She pushed her dark braid back to show her. Sure enough, her ears sloped up into a point before curving down again. "Oh! I almost forgot!" Willow reached into her pocket and pulled out a necklace.

"What's that?"

"It is a crystal necklace." Willow leaned over to show it to her. It was a long crystal that came to a sharp point; the crystal was attached to a thin, silver, twisted metal necklace. "Fayleen asked me to give it to you before you start your training. When we meet her in her study, she will explain." Willow smiled as she tied the necklace on Lane. "There. Now you are ready to begin your training. Let's get this stuff off and get you to your first course."

"I won't need it?"

"I sure hope not."

"AGAIN!"

Lane groaned as Josh barked out the same order over and over again. *Why did Fayleen have to choose Josh as my self-defense teacher?* She thought as she bent over and clenched her knees while panting hard.

Josh sighed in frustration then walked over to her. "Lane, listen. You didn't see any monsters on our way in, but we got lucky. There are creatures out there that can, and will, hurt you. I am here to make sure that doesn't happen. But I can't do that unless you are willing to cooperate." He looked at her sternly, then his eyes slightly softened when he saw how weak and tired she really was. "I also can't do that if you are too exhausted to stand. We can continue this later. As for now, go rest."

Lane nodded, grateful for the break. She stepped out of the training room, and knew as soon as she saw the stretching halls, she was in trouble.

"Ummm ... Josh? How do I get back to my room?"

He simply laughed. "Don't worry. Kinzie can help you. Hey, Kinz!" He called to the young elf as she passed by. "Can you help Lane get back to her room? I need to go check in with Fayleen."

"Of course. That's what I am here for. Willow and Lea are busy with Wizard Fayleen, so I guess you're stuck with me. Let's just hope I can find your room. They all look the same, but perhaps we won't go into the wrong one." She laughed at Lane's horrified expression. "I'm just teasing. In all serious-ness, I *am* here to help you with whatever you need. Let's get on our way." She spun on her heel, and marched off down one of the long halls. Lane had no choice but to trot along with her perky stride.

"There you are!" Kinzie exclaimed as Lane padded out of the bathroom squeezing her hair in one of the fluffy towels she had been provided. "I laid out some clothes for you. I didn't think you would want to go to dinner in a bathrobe," she teased as she focused on the vanity mirror that assisted in the pinning of her hair.

Lane gingerly touched the silver tea gown lying her plush bed. Soft to the touch, the material felt like nothing she had ever seen before.

"Elvantium." Kinzie said, still watching her in the mirror.

"What?"

"Elvantium. It is a type of plant that can be used to make clothes. It is also quite rare. Only found in the Oaken Forest."

"Wow. That's so cool!" Lane exclaimed, impressed.

"Heh, yeah it is. I am just glad I don't have to work with it. It is *extremely* difficult to weave." Kinzie sighed when plac-ing the last pin in her hair bun then she spun around on her stool, and watched as Lane lifted the dress to her shoulders and twirled.

"Go ahead and get dressed," Kinzie said, crossing the room to the door then paused with her hand on the knob, "I'll be back in a few minutes to help you with your hair and jewelry, then we will head down to the Hall for dinner." With those words, she slipped out of the room. Lane took one more look at the dress, and eagerly slipped it over her head.

"Wow! You look beautiful!" Willow exclaimed, slipping through the door, followed by Kinzie and Lea who immediately agreed.

"I have never dreamed of a dress so beautiful!" Lane gushed. A flowing tea gown of silver, with white lace that trimmed the neckline, the bottom of the gown, and the edges of the fitted, elbow-length sleeves.

"Perfect. Well, almost," Willow said, crossing the room to a large jewelry box. She lifted the lid and reached in, carefully removing two dangling crystal earrings. She handed each one to Lane and waited as she slipped them in. Then all four girls climbed up on the bed, Kinzie and Willow each armed with a hair brush. They giggled as they brushed Lane's long hair, though not to any avail. The flowing waves seemed to have a mind of their own. The girls simply let them go as they pleased. No sense in trying to tame the untamable. Lane slid on a pair of silver slippers, and off the girls ran, for they were already late.

The girls came sliding in sideways through the big double doors of The Hall. They were still panting slightly as they slipped into their seats across from Josh and Quinn.

"What took so long?" Josh questioned.

"Don't worry about it," Lane replied with a sly grin at Willow and Kinzie. They tried to stifle their giggles as Josh looked on in suspicion.

"Look! There she is!" Quinn whispered, practically bouncing up and down in his seat, as he pointed to Wizard Fayleen entering The Hall. She stood tall, but you could tell every little thing was wearing down on her. As she reached the end of the long aisle, she slowly turned to face the elves. Everyone waited for her to speak.

"My friends, tonight we celebrate. We celebrate the safe return of two teachers, Josh and Willow, and two students, Lea and Quinn." When the whooping finally died down, Fayleen continued, "And, we also welcome our guest, Alaina Jackson, who will be staying with us for a while. Now, let us begin our celebration with a feast!"

As if on cue, multiple female elves entered, balancing platters stacked high with many different foods. Delectable smells wafted through the air.

"Whoa. That is *a lot* of food," Lane gaped.

"Close your mouth before a dragon flies in it," Josh teased.

Lane laughed as Willow smacked him.

"Dinner *and* a show. This, I could get used to." Quinn giggled, but quickly stopped as Willow turned her stern eyes toward him.

The girls simply laughed.

"Is this what they do all day?" Lane whispered, leaning toward Kinzie.

"Pretty much."

"Wow. Sounds just like my mom and dad-"

But she didn't get a chance to finish, as she slipped out of one world into an entirely different one. A world of memories.

She skipped ahead of her parents, in awe of the office supplies and machinery her parents used every day. She just couldn't stop thinking about how lucky they were to work there.

"One day, I'm going to work here," she told her parents as they caught up with her. Her dad laughed and started to reply, but was cut short by someone screaming. He whipped his head around, and his eyes widened as he saw the plane hurtling toward the building. Her father grabbed her and her mother's hands pulling them away from the windows. Lane heard the squeal of a plane and felt the building shift beneath her as the impact threw them to the floor.

"We have to get out of here!" her father yelled, staggering. He grabbed her hand, but Lane was frozen in horror. "LANE! LANE!"

His voice faded, and was replaced by Willow's.

"Lane? Lane, are you ok?" she asked.

"I-" Lane couldn't finish. She stood and ran out of The Hall, tears filling her eyes.

"Lane?"

Lane looked up from her seat on the floor in one of the many hallways. The last person she expected to come find her, did. Lane sniffled as Josh sat down beside her.

"Lane, what's going on? Does this have something to do with why you left the campsite back at the river? When I mentioned nightmares I had never seen someone look so afraid."

Lane pulled her knees up to her chin and squeezed her eyes shut, trying to hide her tears.

"Lane, talk to me. It's okay. Please tell me what's going on."

Lane tapped her head against the wall then looked over at Josh. Something about seeing him so worried, made her crumble.

"I couldn't save them. I watched them die, and I couldn't save them," Lane sobbed.

At his confused look, she wiped away her tears and started from the beginning.

"My parents worked at a place called the World Trade

Center. They were huge buildings, filled with offices, computers, all kinds of stuff. I loved it there. I had only been a couple of times. That day I got lucky. I got to go to work with my parents for a school assignment. I was so excited to see what they did. I told my parents that when I got older, I was going to work there too. They just grinned, but when my dad started to answer," Lane got choked up, but still managed to continue, "we heard the horrible screams. My dad whipped around to find out what was wrong. That was when we saw it."

"Saw what?" Josh asked cautiously.

Lane wiped away her tears and tried to explain.

"Back where I come from, we have these things called airplanes. They fly people from place to place."

Josh stared in awe. "That sounds like great magic."

Lane tried to smile. "I guess it is magic, in a way, but it didn't seem very magical then." The smile quickly disappeared as she continued her story. "We saw an airplane hurtling toward the building. It had been taken over by terrorists. We tried to run, but … we heard an explosion. The impact threw us to the floor. The first plane had hit the building. All I saw was smoke and flames, and all I heard were screams. My dad grabbed my hand and told me we had to get out. I was frozen, terrified. My dad grabbed my mom's hand and told her we had to get out of the building before things could get any worse. Then he picked me up and started to run, but so did everyone else. Everyone was fighting to get out. I didn't want to see. I closed my eyes and covered my ears, like I was a little girl again. I just couldn't block it out. My dad ran down the stairs with me in his arms, and my mom was right behind us. We finally got down to the bottom level. Many weren't that lucky. I didn't have to see to know that. My dad busted through the doors, frantic to get us out, but my mom wasn't beside us. He looked back at the building, and through the glass, he saw my mom attempting to lift a fallen beam off of a child. My father set me on the concrete, and told me to stay there, but that he had to go back in. He had to help Mom. I cried for him to stay; I didn't want him to leave me. He looked me in the eyes, and told me he had to. He told me he loved me. Then he ran back in to help my mom. As I sat there, I saw them lift the beam. For a second, I thought they were going to make it. They *had* to make it. But then I heard the shriek of another airplane, and saw the second explosion. I heard the people beating on the glass, trying to get out. I saw them jump from the buildings, trying to escape. Then I heard the building moan as it fell crushing all of those people, including my mom and dad."

Lane covered her face and sobbed, not caring who saw her. When she looked over at Josh, he looked just as horror-stricken as she felt.

No holding back now. Tell him, she thought.

"I have flashbacks. It's like- I am back there. I can see it. I can hear the people. And the nightmares are just as bad, if not worse. Back at the dinner table, that was a flashback. I saw my parents, I heard them. And when I snapped out of it, I just-"

She was silenced as Josh wrapped his arms around her. She sobbed into his shoulder.

"Thank you," she whispered, tears slipping down her face.

"Anytime," he replied.

6

MAGIC AND ... MOM?

"ALRIGHT. ARE YOU READY TO BEGIN?" FAYLEEN asked, sitting tall on the couch. Lane looked around Fayleen's study, surprised at what she saw. It was a cozy area, tall book-shelves filled top to bottom with books, both thick and thin. A large brown couch with a beautiful deep brown coffee table in front. A patterned rug on the floor, and warm paintings on the wall.

Lane snapped out of her trance when she saw Fayleen waiting for her answer.

"Oh, um ... yes. Yes, ma'am." Lane replied quickly, blushing.

Fayleen smiled. "Don't worry."

Lane was still a little embarrassed.

Fayleen took a deep breath, then said, "Well. Let's begin."

——⟨◆⟩——

Three hours later, Lane leaned against the wall, sweat dripping down her forehead. "Who would have thought that spells and magic would be harder than self-defense and hand-to-hand fighting."

Fayleen chuckled. "Well, magic is hard work. Some people just can't do it."

"Some people would be me," Lane retorted.

Fayleen smiled gently. "It's alright. It takes time."

"Time that we don't have! From what I hear, people are being hurt. We have to stop it!"

"Yes. We do. But we can't do that unless we work on your magic. You have great potential; I can see it."

"Fine. Let's keep going then," Lane sighed.

Fayleen nodded thoughtfully.

"Such determination. I was the same way when I was young. My parents were too. That's how the portal came to be, and why it has such power."

"What do you mean? What power? I mean, other than being able to transport people from one world to another."

"Well, the Portal is called a magical item. There are many different types. A magical item is associated with a wizard's power. A wizard's name also has a big impact on what power is instilled within that wizard. My mother's name was Juniper, meaning trees. She was the one who created the Portal. My father's name has many meanings, but one of them is 'timekeeper'. My mother created the tree for my father, so he could practice a new spell on it- slowing time. What they didn't know was that my mother's tree was not just a tree. She had created a portal without even knowing it. The spell they thought would slow time here, actually slows time there. What is a day here, is only about a minute there."

"How do you know all of this?"

"Well, experiments. We have tested it. One person goes through for a minute then comes back, and it is a day later here."

"How did someone even think of that? How could someone even think of that possibility?"

"We didn't."

"Then how do you know?"

"I think I have already said too much."

"What do you mean?"

Fayleen looked at her mournfully. "You aren't the only person who has come through that tree."

"Who else did?"

"Lane. I don't think-" Fayleen started.

"Tell me!"

Fayleen sighed, but continued with pain in her voice. "Lane, it was your mom. She was the first one to come through The Tree. We were both teenagers at the time. My parents took Izabella in as one of their own. They trained us together. We became best friends. She came and went, jumping from one world to another. When she would come, she would tell me about the outside world and bring little things for me. Then, as she got older, she came through less and less. On her last journey here, she told me why. She had fallen in love with a man named Isaac Jackson. They were going to be married soon. I had never seen her so happy. I knew that, even though I was going to miss her fiercely, it was best for her. When she left, The Tree disappeared. I waited for it to reappear, but it never did. She never came back."

Lane leaned back in shock.

My mom? And she tells me this now!

"Lane, I understand that this is a bit of a shock-"

"You think?" Lane jumped up and started pacing around the room.

"Listen to me."

Lane stopped pacing and stared at her with panicked eyes.

"When you came here, and I heard your name, I knew exactly who you were."

"And who am I?" Lane cried. "I thought I knew, but now I'm not so sure."

Fayleen stood, and though her body shook, her voice remained steady. "You are Alaina Noel Jackson, daughter of Isaac Jackson and Wizard Izabella Williams. You are capable of more than you know. Much, much more. Magic runs through your veins. It is in your heart. I can see it."

Lane stared at her weakly, afraid of what was coming next.

"You are our only hope. You are the only one who can defeat Witch Hazel, once and for all."

Lane stared at her for a brief moment before she exploded. "Are you *nuts*? I am thirteen years old! I can't defeat a witch! Especially not one who is known for nearly defeating you, the most powerful wizard alive!"

"Lane-" Fayleen began.

"No! Are you *insane*?"

"Possibly, but-"

"No way!"

"Lane-"

"This is can't be happening. Please tell me this is not happening." Lane's voice shook.

"Lane, breathe. Calm down."

"I just realized my mom was here and was a wizard! Do you not see that this is more than a tiny bit far-fetched?"

"Yes, I do. Trust me. This isn't easy for me either. I don't know why the tree reappeared for you, or why you are here, or why you came when you did. But it did, and all the questions but the last, have obvious answers. You have wizardry in your blood, so the tree appeared for you as it should. I truly believe that you are here to help us."

Lane laid her head against the wall.

"That's not possible!" she insisted.

"Many things have happened that I once believed to be impossible. Yet, they have happened. It was impossible for Witch Hazel to wake up. It was impossible for her monsters to break the protective barrier. It was impossible that a tree could have the power to transport a person from one world to another. It was impossible for a human child to learn magic. But here we are. Witch Hazel is awake. Her monsters are attacking villages. My parents built a portal. And your mother, a human child, learned magic, and became an amazing wizard. I believe that you can too."

"I-" Lane's eyes filled with tears. "I just can't."

Lane fled the room.

—◈—

Willow, Kinzie, and Lea walked in the shared bedroom laughing, but quickly stopped when they saw Lane lying in bed with the covers pulled up to her chin, eyes closed.

Willow smiled and whispered to the others, "It *is* late. I can't blame her. We need to get to bed too, but be quiet. She needs to sleep."

They simply nodded, not wanting to wake Lane.

A few minutes later, Lane rolled over and opened one of her eyes. When she was sure that they were all sound asleep, she pushed away the covers and slid out of bed in full dress. She tightened the straps on one of her fingerless gloves, smiling as she remembered laughing with Willow while picking out her clothes.

Maybe I should stay … Lane looked over at the girls sleeping. As quickly as the thought came, she shook her head with determination. No. I can't stay here. I can't help them. I have to go.

She silently pulled her backpack from under the bed and slipped it over her shoulders, tightened her belt where her small sword hung, made sure her matching daggers were still safe in the hidden flaps in the inside of her knee-high boots, and pulled the hood of her waist-length brown cape over her head. I'm ready to go.

She tip-toed over to the door, hoping the giant oak wouldn't creak. She slowly turned the handle- click! Lane froze, but breathed sigh of relief when she realized it was just the tiny mechanism opening the door. She slowly pushed it open. Halfway through the door, she stopped and turned to look back at her friends lying sound asleep. She smiled wanly, thinking about how much she would miss her them, then she quietly closed the door. This time when it clicked, she was on the other side.

Lane breathed a sigh of relief. Step one, done. Now I just have to get the rest of the way out of the castle. She looked around at the eerily lit hallway. Torches were mounted on the walls with the flames dancing about, casting shadows here and there; it blanketed her with a foreboding sensation. She shook her head, trying to get the image out of her mind. Stay focused! I've got to get out of here. She looked both ways to make sure no one was coming and took off in a silent run. As she ran, she tried to remember how to get back to The Tree.

I'll go through the woods for a few miles, then I should arrive at the river. I'll stop there for a few hours, then I'll keep going straight until I hit the fields. I should be able to see Evoron Hills from there, then hike where The Tree is. Easy. Assuming I can make it that far without running into any monsters.

She paused at a corner just a few yards from the doors. She peeked around, making sure no one was guarding them, then padded over. She put her shoulder up against one of the ginormous oak doors and pushed as hard as she could. Wincing as it groaned open, Lane continued to slink through, then slowly pulled it closed.

UH-OH. She quickly hid behind a pillar and held her breath as two guards walked by on their nightly rounds. In her rush to fill her pack and plan her route, there was one thing she had forgotten. The GATE! She remembered Lea and Quinn showing her the castle, and telling her all the proper names. Apparently, Metal Thingy was not the proper term. The large cast iron gate was quite intimidating at first, but the name made it quite comical instead. A Yett they called it.

They laughed quite a lot going through all the names. Lane smiled wistfully at the castle. No, she scolded herself. I can't stay. I don't belong here. But she couldn't quite convince herself. She worked up her courage and peeked around the edge of the pillar. As the guard rounded the far corner of the castle, Lane sprinted to the yett. She hoped and prayed the squares would be big enough for her to squeeze through before the guards showed up again. She tossed her backpack through to the other side, then wiggled herself through one of the openings. For once, being tiny is a good thing. She scooped up her backpack and fled into the dark, dense forest.

7

ᴡITCHES AND ᴡOLVES

Lane ran through the forest, dodging trees, trying to put as much distance as she could between herself and the Crystal Castle. She stopped and doubled over out of breath. With her hands on her knees, she took in her surroundings. What caught her eye the most were the trees. Large, bulbous trees with ivy woven through their branches.

That would be the perfect place to stop for the night. I can climb up, and the ivy should keep me pretty well hidden.

She got to work. First, she had to figure out how to get her backpack into the tree.

Ivy! The answer was right in front of me!

She pulled down three thick strands and got to work braiding. Apparently, those lessons from Lea weren't so worthless after all. Once she had a thick rope, she threw it over one of the lowest hanging on the tall branches and tied the other end to the backpack.

"Now to get *me* up," she whispered, a thought taking hold. "I could use ivy again, but I don't know if it would hold. Did I put rope in my bag?" *I should have checked for that before I used the ivy.*

She rummaged through her backpack and found quite the assortment of items. Matches, a jacket, a blanket, food, first aid bandages, her mom's diary … all very important, but no rope. She looked around, her frown deepening. *Maybe I don't need rope at all.* She looked down at the small sword dangling from her belt and was struck with an idea. She ripped out her sword and swung at the tree angling downward; she pulled it back out and swung a little lower with the blade horizontal this time. She smiled in triumph when large chunk fell out. Her first foot hole. She repeated this process starting high, and going lower. When she had completed this task, she pulled two daggers out of their sheaths. She plunged her dagger into the tree a few feet above the first hole. She placed the end of her right boot in the first hole and lifted herself off the ground. She repeated the process with her left, pulled out the right dagger, and stabbed the tree above the next hole smiling as she climbed onto the first branch. When she reached it, she wrapped an arm around the trunk then heaved herself up onto the next branch. She pulled up her backpack and slung it over her shoulders. As Lane looked up, she saw that she had not climbed an average tree. It looked full from the outside, almost like an ivy-covered globe; but on the inside, it was hollow. It had a few low branches; but when you got up into the tree, it was completely empty, with the exception of the tree trunk standing in the center as a support. The leaves were tightly knit together to create a flat, firm floor with a curved ceiling and walls. She cautiously stepped on the floor and breathed a sigh of relief when it didn't move. She walked across the room and knelt on the floor as she dug through her bag. She drew out a thick blanket and spread it on the floor. This would serve as a mattress. Lane then pulled out another to use as a cover. She smiled thoughtfully as she remembered how Willow and Lea had explained the pack's unique qualities when they gave it to her.

"It's called a Moonbeam Pack. It is made out of Shining Silver, woven out of the silver leaves of a Moonbeam plant," Lea had explained.

"What is a Moonbeam plant?" Lane asked.

"It is an extremely rare plant, only found on Amaryllis Isle. It gets its name for two reasons. Number one, its bloom shines silver at night just like the moon, a truly gorgeous sight. Number two, the leaves on it stretch and contract like light itself. When woven together in a pack, you can put as many items as you wish in, and it will never run out of space, never get larger, and never get heavy. It will always be as light as if it had nothing in it," Willow told her. "When you want to summon an item, stick your hand in your bag and think about the item you want. It won't work if you haven't put the item in there in the first place, so try to keep track of what you have."

"That is so cool!" Lane had said, getting excited.

Lane smiled at the memory then looked back down at her bag and plunged both hands in. When she pulled them out, she had a small wooden box in one and her mom's diary in the other. She placed the diary on the floor and just stared at the box. After taking a deep breath, she gently pushed the lid back and pulled out its treasure. A small crystal dangled from a thin leather lace. She examined the silver one around her neck. *Almost exactly the same. With just one difference.* One was from Fayleen, the other was her mom's. She had found the necklace in the small wooden box in her mom's old room pushed behind her diary covered in dust. Lane lay on the blanket and pulled up her covers, her mother's necklace held tightly in hand. Smiling at her mother's memory, she slowly drifted to sleep.

———

Smoke, flames, screaming …

Lane sat up in a cold sweat. She lay back on her blanket with her hands covering her face.

CRACK!

Lane froze as she heard a twig snap on the ground below her. She slowly rolled over, and looked down, barely containing a scream. Through the thickly woven leaves and branches, she saw below her a slim figure dressed in black with a hood pulled over her head. A massive, white, wolf-like creature stood beside the woman, its fiery eyes trained on her waiting expectantly for orders. The hooded figure stood in front of it placing thin, pale hands on each side of the creature's thick head.

"Go, find what I want. Do my bidding; do not fail me." Her high-pitched whisper pierced the air. The sound was not loud, but it made the blood freeze in Lane's veins.

She watched in horror as the creature closed its eyes,

tilted back its head, and howled. She covered her ears at the deafening sound. The giant ashen creature was immediately surrounded by at least a dozen more, these all black. Some were the size of a horse, others the size of a large wolf. The shadowy figure looked around at her troop then stared into the distance. She lifted her arm, her cape falling back to reveal pasty white skin and long black nails. She tightened her hand in a fist with one bony finger pointing out.

"Go," her voice rasped.

As the dark, menacing beasts sped off like lightning, the white one stayed behind. The woman looked at him, and he knelt to her. She walked around to his side, and sat on him as one might sit on a horse. Which was a pretty good analogy, seeing that he was as big as one.

Lane stared, frozen in fear as she watched them speed off into the night.

8

CORAL AND COMING BACK

LANE BEGAN TO BREATHE MORE EASILY AS THEY disappeared.

I have to get out of here.

Lane got busy. She rolled off of her blanket and started gathering everything. She slid her blankets, the small wooden box, and the diary all in her backpack. She crawled across the floor and peeked down through the hole she had climbed up in.

Well, this is going to be interesting.

Lane tried to measure the distance between herself and

the hard ground. A minor fall, only about eight feet, but a fall none the less.

The last thing Grandma and Grandpa are going to want to see when I come home, is a broken leg and no explanation.

Lane grabbed her backpack, swiftly unwinding the ivy rope. With one end still attached to the branch, Lane could only hope it would hold her. She finished tying it around herself and grabbed her backpack. Lane dropped her backpack gently, but the loud crunch still made her wince.

I just hope I don't crunch too.

"Owww," Lane moaned as she rubbed her backside.

That rope probably should have been a few feet shorter.

She stood up and brushed herself off. Then she scooped up her backpack and hurried into the woods. Lane ran panting through the trees.

She stopped for a moment to catch her breath and perceived the calming sound of rushing water. She looked around and smiled at what she saw. She was standing in their old campsite. There were the remains of the fire with stones lined around it. There lay the crowns Lane and Lea had woven out of ivy and dandelions. Well, something like dandelions. Here, they were white like a star, and they smelled differently.

Lea had explained and called them Wishing Stars. "You think of a memory, or something you miss; and when you smell the flowers, that is what they smell like." Her voice still rang loud in Lane's ears.

Lane picked up a crown and pulled out one of the Stars. She smelled it and smiled. "It smells like the baking bread in The Hall back at the castle," Lane whispered, her eyes closed and her hands clung to the flower. She slipped it into her bag promising herself that, when she got home, she would press it in a book. She stood up and started walking toward the river, then stumbled over something in the grass. She knelt, and when she brushed the grass away-

"My camera!" Lane exclaimed, then quickly covered her mouth, looking around. "My camera!" she whispered more quietly but just as excited. "I didn't even notice it was gone!"

She pressed the power button and almost squealed when it came on. Lane stood up, walked over to the river, and perched herself on the large flat rock. As she started flipping through the pictures, she started to grin. There was a picture of her with the fairies in the woods. One of her and Lea making the crowns and talking. Willow making supper and scolding Josh and Quinn for trying to sneak biscuits. The beautiful sunset, illuminating the rippling water with an assortment of blues, pinks, oranges, and colors that could not be named for their beauty. A picture of Coral. And then she started getting into the pictures of home. There she was with her grandpa at the lodge. With her grandma in the kitchen. Sleeping with Davy on the couch.

Hm. Grandpa must have snuck my camera. That solves the mystery of why I woke up with dog hair all over me. She sighed but kept flipping through. The picture from the car on the way to the lodge, the trees and the mountains. At the airport meeting her new guardians, and-

Her parents. Holding hands at the World Trade Center. Walking around with Lane, showing her things that Lane could use for her report. A picture of her parents at home that morning; mom making breakfast and dad reading the paper. Lane started crying, her hands shaking so badly she dropped the camera with a thud in the river sand. But she didn't care. She dropped her backpack on the ground and launched herself off the rock. She started pacing, her hands on her head, sobs racking her body.

"Why?" she whispered. "Why not take me instead? Why would You do this to me?" Lane cried staring at the sky. "Why would You take everything from me? Why don't You just come show me the way?" Her voice cracked. "I don't know what to do," Lane whispered, falling to her knees. She ripped off the necklace Fayleen had given her, and threw it in the river out of frustration. Warm tears slipped down her cheeks.

"Well, I'm not God, and I can't answer all your questions; but I may be able to give you a little advice," came a sweet voice from the river.

Lane jerked back flailing her arms as she fell on her rear, scrambling to get away from the river. Coral chuckled slightly but stayed where she was.

"Don't do that!" Lane gasped, her hand on her heart. "You scared the living daylights out of me!" she said trying to wipe the tears away before Coral could see them.

"Alaina, I don't know how long I will be here according to the rumors."

"What do you mean?"

"Witch Hazel. She is awake and on the move."

"On the move to where?"

"Anywhere and everywhere. She is out for vengeance. She will try to destroy Fayleen and then The Forest along with all its inhabitants. Everyone is trying to escape, but they don't know where to go. The Forest used to be the safest place for everyone. But now ..." Coral didn't need to finish.

"What can we do?"

"No, no. Not *we*. *You*."

"She is *witch*. I am just a *kid*. *Why does no one get that!*" Lane exclaimed. "I am no hero!"

"Alaina. You are not just a kid. You are the daughter of Wizard Izabella Williams, the greatest wizard this world has ever known. She was greater than King Neilan and Queen Juniper. You have her blood in you. The blood of a wizard. But that doesn't matter." Coral let that sink in. "You say you tried using magic, and it didn't work. Do you really think it matters that you failed trying to move water from a pitcher into a glass without your hands? No. You say you are no hero? Being a hero is not defined by who a person is or a person's bloodline. It is a choice. You can choose to be the hero. You can choose which side to be on. You can choose to leave and never look back. Or, you can choose to stay and fight for us. You can be the hero."

"So, you are saying I should go back?"

"I am saying it is your choice. You do what you think is right. No one can force you to do anything. You have free will."

"What if I make the wrong choice? What if I fail?"

"No one is perfect, Alaina. You think your mother got every spell right every time? I can assure you, she didn't. She made mistakes, but she didn't give up. She worked hard. She was courageous. That is why she was great. That's why she was our hero."

"So you *are* saying go back. I don't know. I am not exactly very courageous. Honestly, I'm scared."

"I am saying, don't give up because it is hard. But, it's up to you. It is your choice. You will be able to do what you need to do when the time arises. I can assure you of that."

Lane sprinted through the woods, pausing only for a few minutes when out of breath. She started to worry she wouldn't get there in time when she saw the sun start to rise, but she was relieved to see the Green Flag waving high on the guard tower. She smiled at the crisscrossed tree in the middle of it. As she scurried to the yett she plastered herself to the wall waiting for the guard to pass by. Then Lane wriggled through the gate and hurried into the castle.

She looked up and down the halls to make sure no one was coming and then padded down the corridor toward her room.

"Lane?"

She froze and slowly turned around.

"Lane, I have been looking everywhere for you! Where have you been?" Willow scolded, wrapping her arms around her in a hug.

"I um …" Lane wondered how much she should say.

"Oh, don't worry about it now. We have to go," Willow said, pulling her along.

"Go? Go where?"

"Haven't you heard? It's Fayleen! She has gotten worse. Much, much worse. She is so weak, she can barely speak. The entire castle has been awake for hours trying to find anything that would help, but she refuses everything. She just asks for you," Willow explained, hurrying Lane down the hall to Fayleen's room.

"Why? Why would she want me?"

"Beats me. Why don't you ask her yourself?" Willow said pushing a large door open. Lane stepped into the dimly lit room. There were many elves bustling about trying to find something, anything, that could help, but Lane somehow had a feeling that there was no hope for Fayleen. She tiptoed over to Fayleen's bedside and almost cried at the sight. Fayleen's hair was thin, her skin as white as snow, and eyes were barely cracked open.

"Fayleen?" Lane whispered.

"Lane? Is that you?" Fayleen said in a hoarse whisper, weakly placing her hand on Lane's.

"It's me. What happened?" Lane asked, biting her lip to keep the tears away.

"I get weaker as she gets stronger. Before long, she will be too powerful to take down." Fayleen whispered. Just talking sent her into a coughing fit. Lane grabbed another pillow and placed it behind her back.

"Who?" Lane asked, but already knowing the answer.

"Witch Hazel. She is coming. I know it. I can feel it."

"We have to stop her then," Lane said, determined, and ready to fight.

"No."

That stopped Lane cold.

"What?"

"No. You can't go after her now. She's too strong. I see how foolish I was to ask of you such a thing."

"I want to try."

"Lane. Your mother-"

"Would tell me to do what's right. That's exactly what she would do, and you know it. I am going to fight. I am going to stay and protect what I have learned to love." Lane started to pace with determination, then continued, "I will be courageous. When no one else stands, I will. When no one will fight the battle between good and evil, I will. When no one is willing to be the hero-"

Lane stopped, and turned to face the Wizard.

"I will."

9

FAIRIES TO FIGHT FOR

"YOUR MAJESTY!" JOSH CRIED BURSTING INTO THE
study. He stopped when he saw Lane with her hands outstretched, concentrating. He folded his hands and waited
patiently.

Lane dropped her hands, and swiveled around to face him.

"I am having a hard time concentrating anyway, so go
ahead. I could use some good news."

"Prepare to be disappointed," Josh replied. Lane knew
something was gravely wrong when she heard his tone.

"Your Majesty," he continued, "we have a situation. There
has been an attack."

Lane gasped, and Josh's grim look told her that the news was going to get even worse.

"It was Kymn village. Witch Hazel and her beasts have destroyed everything. The houses, the gardens, everything. It's gone."

"Wait, the Kymn village? Rosie, Jules, and Oakley's *home*?" Lane asked, horrified.

Josh nodded, a pained expression on his face.

"It's also the largest populated fairy village. We just got the report; my men and I are about to go check on it now."

"Let me go with you. Please," Lane begged him.

"You aren't ready."

"I am going. I don't care if I am ready or not. I'm going. End of story."

Lane pushed past him and through the door.

Josh shot a look at Fayleen, but she was gazing out the window.

"Your Majesty-"

"Josh, let her go. Let her see. Just … keep a very close eye on her. I don't want anything to happen to her."

"Yes, your Majesty," Josh replied bowing. As he closed the door, he sighed. He wasn't happy with the decision, but he knew they were both right. Lane must see for herself.

Lane hurried to keep stride with the group of elves surging through The Forest as they neared the village. As they fell through the tree line into the rolling fields, they all stopped abruptly to stare in horror.

The lush hills, usually a bright green, were gray with

ash. The gardens that were once filled with exceeding crops, were now nothing but black dirt and trampled vegetables. The orchards were nothing but bare, burning trees. But the most painful were the houses. The large village that had been filled with brightly-colored, miniature-sized houses, was now burned a coal black and trampled into splinters. Some still had flames leaping from the rooftops. As they approached the village Josh started dividing his people into groups. A group to find the fairies, one to check the orchards and gardens, and another to go through the houses.

"Lane, come on. You're with me," Josh said. "We will look for the fairies."

Josh pulled his bow off his back and notched an arrow. Lane drew her daggers from her boots and closely followed behind him.

"We need to look around the tree line first. Start where we came in and circle around."

Lane nodded mutely.

They went back up the hill and began walking along the tree line. They stayed barely inside the trees, far enough to see into the thick forest and still view the fields. As they slowly trekked along, Lane spotted a faint glimmer at the bottom of a tree. She tapped Josh's arm and pointed to the tree. Lane peeked inside a gap in the tree and was heartbroken at what she saw. The hollow fit about twenty fairies, all under a foot tall. They were packed side by side around bottom edge of the hollow. They gazed up at her, and she could see how scared they were.

"It's alright," Lane whispered. "You can come out. You are safe now." She stepped back and watched as they hesitantly climbed out. They stayed together in a tight group, but one stepped away emitting a loud, clear whistle. Out of twenty or more trees, fairies emerged. Lane looked around. There were children less than six inches tall, babies only a few inches long, and adults about a foot tall. They all gathered into one large group and stared at Josh and Lane. Josh got down on his knees and motioned for Lane to do the same so she could be slightly closer to the fairies' size.

Josh cleared his throat and started to speak to them. "Hi. I'm Josh. This is Lane." Lane waved at them, and a few of them smiled and waved back. Josh continued, "We are here to help you. We are going to take you to the Crystal Palace. I would like to ask you some questions before we go. Is that okay?"

They looked amongst each other and nodded nervously.

Josh breathed a little easier knowing this wasn't going to be as difficult as expected. He took a deep breath and began. "Who did this?"

A few fairies murmured among themselves, but one of them stepped forward to reply.

"The witch and her beasts," he said, glancing around nervously as if they might come pouncing out of the woods any second.

"Beasts?" Josh asked, confused.

"Wait a minute," Lane said, putting the pieces together. "Were these beasts very big, black coat, long snout, red eyes, long claws, anything like that?"

They all nodded, but Lane kept going.

"Was the witch wearing all black, with pale skin and long black nails? Was she riding the biggest of the monsters, this one white with red eyes and big fangs?" Lane questioned, scared of the answer.

Again, to Lane's dismay, they all nodded; and one of them announced, "Howlhounds."

Josh pulled her aside. "How did you know that?"

"Last night, I left the castle. I was trying to go home. I stayed in a tree and fell asleep, but a snapping sound woke me up. When I rolled over and looked down, I saw a woman in long black robes. I never saw her face, but when she looked at a white wolf-like creature, I heard her voice. She told it, 'Do what I ask, go find what I seek, and do not fail me.' Then that thing, whatever it was, let out a huge howl and black ones came. They took off running, and the woman climbed up on the white one and raced off after the black ones. I got scared, so I climbed down out of the tree and took off. I found myself at the river, found my camera, talked to Coral, and changed my mind about going home. That is when I heard about Fayleen, and you know the story from there." Lane took in a deep breath of air and looked at Josh. He may as well have been a statue from his expression. Then, he blew up.

"YOU DID WHAT!" Josh yelled.

"Well ..." Lane looked down at her feet.

"You could have gotten killed! What were you thinking?"

"That my now-dead mom turned out to be a wizard. That I had to kill a witch. That my life was falling apart! I wanted to go home!" Lane cried.

That shut Josh up for a moment. Then he responded. "Why didn't you just tell me?"

"You wouldn't have understood." A lone tear slipped down her face.

"When I was a child, I lost my entire family in an attack from Witch Hazel's monsters. Fayleen took me in. That is why I was placed in the castle for training. I was told it was my job to protect the kingdom. I am pretty sure I understand perfectly," Josh said.

Lane was taken aback. "Josh-"

But Josh was upset, frustrated, and did not want to talk to Lane. He turned around to face the fairies. At their frightened little faces, he softened.

"Come on. Let's get you to the castle," Josh said gently.

"**What** happened?" Willow asked, running into the courtyard as the troop arrived with the fairies. When no one answered, she went up to Lane, but Willow was quickly silenced when Lea clamped a hand over her mouth. Lea gestured for her to be quiet, and then showed her a small, bulging blanket in Lane's arms. Lane lowered part of it to reveal seven sleeping baby fairies.

"I'll tell you in a minute," Lane mouthed.

Willow nodded in understanding.

Willow pushed against the heavy door. Lane winced as it creaked loudly, but she stepped through anyway. A small group of elves hurried over to them, and Lea left with them to lead the fairies into the wing of the castle they would be staying in. One of the women stayed behind, her arms outstretched for the blanket Lane was holding. Lane reluctantly handed them over. Lane sighed as she watched them leave. Willow waited patiently for her to explain, but she wasn't quite ready.

"Sooo ..." Willow asked pressingly.

Lane took a deep breath. "The village, the gardens, the orchards; everything is gone. Destroyed. *Trampled.* And I know who did it." She started marching to the armory but stopped and turned to face Willow. "And I am going to stop it."

In the armory, Lane tightened the third strap on the side of her stiff, leather chest plate and slipped her small sword into its sheath. *Now the hard part. Getting permission from Fayleen.* Lane lightly jogged down the hallway to the thick oak door at the entrance to Fayleen's room. She placed her shoulder up against it and pushed. She stepped in but was stopped by the sobs. There were all her friends, and a few more, gathered around Fayleen's bed.

"No," Lane whispered. She hurried forward, pushing her way through. Fayleen lay unmoving, and from where Lane stood, she could barely hear the short, shallow breaths. Lane turned to face her friends.

"W-what happened?" Lane asked, scared of the answer. "Is she-"

"No, no. She is just sleeping now, but I don't think-" Willow couldn't finish.

Josh picked up where she left off. "We honestly don't know what's going on. We know she has been getting weaker, and I fear she is close to the end. I don't think there is anything we can do."

Lane stopped, struck with an idea.

"Josh, can I speak with you outside for a minute?" Lane asked.

"Um …sure, I guess," he replied, hesitant to leave Fayleen.

Lane grabbed his arm and practically dragged him out the door. When they were outside, Lane checked both ways to make sure no one was coming.

"What if we stopped it?"

"Stopped what? There is nothing we can do for Fayleen."

"I don't just mean Fayleen. I mean the attacks, too. What if I stopped Witch Hazel?"

Josh stepped back as if struck. "What! Are you *out of your mind?*"

"Uh, maybe. But I'm serious. What if I stopped her?"

"That's crazy!"

Lane started to reply, but Josh continued, "But it might just be crazy enough to work."

10

COURAGE AND CONFRONTATION

JOSH AND LANE QUIETLY SLINKED THROUGH THE woods, Josh's bow shaking nervously but readily, and Lane's hand tensely clenching her mother's crystal necklace. Lane remembered her sweet smile, her laugh, her eyes filled with love. Lane dashed a hand at her filling eyes. *Focus, Lane.*

"I still can't believe we convinced Willow to let us go," Josh whispered.

"I can't either," Lane replied just as quietly. She started to say more but was interrupted by a loud *SNAP!*

Josh pulled her behind a tree and pinned her arms against it, holding her in place.

"SHHHH!" Josh scolded. "What did I say about watching where you step?"

"It wasn't me!" Lane protested, wriggling out of his grasp.

Josh's eyes widened in horror at what that must mean. Lane was puzzled at his expression, until ... They both whirled around to face whoever was behind them. And there, before them, was Witch Hazel. She was clad in a long black dress, and a long black cloak trailed behind her. Lane could not see her face, for her long black hood fell down over it. She patted the top of the howlhound's head and slid off his back. The howlhound snarled at them, and Lane stepped back, terrified. Josh drew his bow, but Witch Hazel threw up a hand. Lane braced herself for a spell; but when she cracked her eyes, she was surprised. Hazel placed her head against the howlhound's sloped forehead and whispered to it. It slowly lay down but kept a wary eye on them. Josh remained strong, his bow drawn.

But the Witch simply laughed, the sweet sound grating on Lane's nerves.

"Oh children, children. Lower your weapons. We are not here to hurt you." The Witch lifted her pale, bony hands and threw back her hood. Lane was surprised at the sight before her. Not at all how she pictured a witch. This woman was enchantingly beautiful, with long, silky, raven hair that drifted over her shoulders and down her back to her waist. She had extremely pale skin. Her eyes were so deep of a brown, that, at first glance, they appeared to be black. She smiled, and her teeth where as white as the moon. Lane started to loosen her hold on her necklace, and she watched as Josh slowly lowered his bow to his side. The Witch smiled encouragingly and eagerly-

Too eagerly. Her guard instantly went back up.

"If you aren't trying to hurt us, what do you want? Why would you send your armies against us and our friends?" Lane attempted to speak bravely, but it came out as more of a squeak. It was all Lane needed to say to shake Josh out of his trance. His grip tightened on his bow. Witch Hazel's smile seemed more forced as she realized sweet tones were not going to help her.

"What I want, only you can give. Your necklace. Give it to me."

Lane was stunned at her request. She glanced over at Josh for an explanation, but he looked just as confused. Suddenly, she remembered something Fayleen had said about names. Everything about a wizard has power. Even their names ... it dawned on her.

"Wait, it's a crystal. Fayleen *Crystal*."

The Witch cringed at the name, but Lane did not stop.

"If you have a crystal, you think you can duplicate her spells and fix your creatures. Maybe even take over the Forest like you tried before. But Fayleen stopped you, didn't she?" Lane watched as the anger and bitterness fleeted over the woman's face. "She placed you under a sleep spell with only slight consciousness. But it was flawed. Only slightly, but it was just enough for you to plan and scheme your way out. You must have planned for years. And now you are free, but you are also afraid. Afraid that a little girl just *might* have the power to defeat you. Just like Fayleen did." Lane tried to stall her, attempting to find a mental loophole in her plan. She got exactly what she needed.

"Yes!" Witch Hazel screeched, her eyes morphing into a fiery red and flaming orange. "I mean, no!" Her eyes quickly changed back, but her voice wavered a little before she quickly regained, but not soon enough. Lane had found her soft spot, and she had seen her true form. Lane stepped in front of Josh. He grabbed her arm to pull her back, but she brushed him aside.

"What do you want? Attention?" Realization dawned. "Your parents always favored Fayleen. They chose her over you. Well, that makes sense. She is good. Unlike you." Lane pressed, trying to get her to crack. She got what she wanted.

"STOP!" Hazel cried out, stumbled, and fell to her knees covering her ears.

"No! What are you going to do with the crystal? Destroy Fayleen? The Forest? Me?"

"STOP!" Witch Hazel screamed. A chill swept across the forest causing Lane's blood to freeze in her veins. Josh quickly stepped forward and pushed Lane behind him, drawing his bow protectively. Lane fell back onto the hard ground. Witch Hazel rose and glowered down at them. The howlhound backed up. Even he knew that, when she was mad, she was not one to be reckoned with.

"Silly boy," she spat. She thrust forth her hand disintegrating his bow on the spot, then grabbed Josh with some unseen force. He was lifted into the air, writhing in pain before being thrown against a tree. He rolled across the ground and lay there unmoving.

"Josh!" Lane screamed.

Witch Hazel shook her finger at him and tsked. "This is not your fight," she scolded him, her voice cruel and cold. She whirled around to face Lane who scooted backwards into a tree. "Now, little girl, are you afraid? You have seen but a mere glimpse of my power. I can do so much more," she threatened. "I think it is time to give me that crystal. Do you really think that you will hold out over a witch? You will fear me!" she thundered.

Lane was completely terrified, but she looked up calmly and spoke with a strength not her own.

"Courage is not living without fear. It is looking fear in the eye. It is fighting through life no matter what it throws at you. It is *overcoming* fear." She clenched her necklace even tighter, pushed herself off the ground into a standing position, and continued, "Am I afraid? Of course. But *you* are the one who should be."

"Fine. I guess I will just have to kill you then." Witch Hazel's hands filled with a swirling black mist. She shoved her hands forward, and the mist shot toward Lane.

Time seemed to slow for Lane. Closing her eyes, she whispered a prayer that this would work. She thought of the fairies, the dwarves, the kind elves at the castle, the silverfins in the river, Coral, her grandparents in Tennessee, and last, but not least, her parents. She remembered the strength and courage they had. Lane started to feel her energy boost and her heart quicken. She felt the power flow from the center of her chest, all throughout her body.

She opened her eyes and almost stumbled from surprise. A white glow seemed to cover her body, almost like a protective bubble. The dark mist could not touch her. She raised her head and met Witch Hazel's fiery eyes. She saw Hazel staring in shock and horror. Lane saw that she was afraid. Maybe that would work to her advantage. *Maybe I won't have to fight at all.*

"Leave. Leave and never return, or fight a battle you cannot win."

Witch Hazel recovered from her shock and let out a bloodcurdling scream hurtling herself at Lane. Lane thrust forth her hands and spoke the only word she could think of.

"SLEEP!"

Witch Hazel crumpled on the spot. Lane eased forward cautiously, and almost laughed when she heard her snore. She looked down at her hands, held them out palms up, and slowly lifted them. She watched as Witch Hazel floated. Lane closed her eyes and pictured the Mist Mountains in the distance. She pictured a dark cave with a room carved in solid stone; one with no doors, no windows, and no way of escape. *Please work, please work, please work.* When she opened her eyes, Witch Hazel was gone, and Lane was the only person who knew where she was. She looked around; there was no sign of the howlhound either. Serenity slowly enveloped her in its warm blankets, and peace flowed over her like a waterfall.

Suddenly, Lane remembered.

"Josh!" Lane yelled, looking around. She stopped when she saw him laying by the tree. She ran to him and gasped at his broken body. He was bruised and mangled, and a large gash on his forehead openly flowed blood. She placed her hand on his arm and could feel the pain coursing throughout his body. She closed her eyes and focused, searching for a heartbeat.

THERE!

Lane nearly shouted for joy when she felt his heart beat. It was small and weak, but it was still there. Lane placed one hand on his chest and the other on his forehead. She remembered all the times they had. She smiled as she felt the warmth flow from her chest to her fingertips and into Josh's body. When she opened her eyes, she gasped. He lay there, completely healed, with only a long, thin, pink scar on the right side of his forehead stopping just above his eyebrow. Lane closed her eyes and breathed a sigh of relief.

"So, is she gone?"

Lane yelped, flailed her arms, and fell back on her rear end. Josh laughed, trying to sit up. Lane clutched her chest, gasping.

"Don't do that!" she said, smacking his arm.

"Sorry, but seriously, is she gone?" Josh said glancing about nervously, as if waiting for her to jump out from behind a tree any second.

"Gone," Lane replied. "And she is never going to hurt anyone again."

"No, she won't."

Josh and Lane both whirled around. There stood an old man with white hair, wearing tanned leather pants and moccasins, with a white wolf's pelt draped over his bare back and shoulders.

Josh quickly knelt, and Lane did the same, even though she had no clue who this strange man was.

The old man chuckled. "Do not bow to me. It is I, who should bow to you. You set me free from the spell. So long I have been trapped, searching for a way out. I was forced to do as she commanded; the things I have seen and done ..." The man shook his head.

"Wait, you were the white howlhound?" Lane said, shocked.

"Yes, my dear. But I am no longer bound by the wicked witch's spells. I am Omah, Lord of the Hunters, and we are free."

Lane looked around, and they were surrounded by many men in similar clothing. These were younger men, some still appeared to be in their teens, with black wolf pelts on their own bare shoulders, and a few were barefoot.

"You freed us, and now, we thank you."

Each of the men each knelt, and lastly, Omah did.

"Now, we must go. But I believe, one day, we will meet again."

They all took off sprinting into the woods with Omah at the front of the pack. As old as he appeared, he was as spry as any of the young men, and had no problem leading them.

Josh looked at Lane, shocked. Lane stared after them. Then Josh jumped up and whooped. He picked her up and swung her around, yelling. She laughed out loud.

"I knew you could do it!" he said capturing Lane in a hug. "You defeated Witch Hazel, and then you freed the Lord of The Hunters? Seriously?"

"Ok, ok. That's enough." Lane giggled, pushing him away. "We need to get back to the Crystal Castle. Then we can celebrate."

"Even if we walk all night, it would be tomorrow morning when we arrive. The sun is setting now, and it took us hours just to get here!"

"I have a shortcut," Lane smiled. Before Josh could say anything, Lane slipped her hand in his, and thought of the castle's stretching courtyards, colorful gardens, and the sweet smell of the flowers. She smiled as she started to feel the warmth spread from her chest outward.

Josh gasped as he opened his eyes to view the Crystal Castle Courtyard. Josh turned stared at her. Lane blushed.

"What?"

"That ... Was ... AMAZING!"

Lane just laughed.

It feels good to finally laugh. Lane smiled.

"So, does this mean you can sneak me and Quinn into the Castle's pantry any time?"

"No."

"Well, it was worth a shot."

A smart comeback had just come to mind when Willow hastened around the edge of the Castle. She gasped, but quickly recovered from her surprise and ran to embrace them both tightly.

"So ... what happened?" Willow asked. Her eyes widened when she saw the pale pink scar down Josh's forehead. She started to ask, but Lane shook her head.

"I'll explain later. For now, how is Fayleen?"

Willow's eyes started to fill. "She doesn't have very long."

"I thought defeating Witch Hazel would cure her!" Lane cried.

"Lane, it wasn't just Witch Hazel. The strain of caring for The Forest has taken its toll on her. Just like it will for the next Wizard, whoever that may be. Though I may have a guess."

"Who?" Lane asked.

"Well ..." Willow looked at her.

"*Me?*" Lane squeaked.

"I don't know. But maybe," Willow said thoughtfully.

"No! I have to go home! I have grandparents waiting for me on the other side of the tree! I can't stay and be a wizard! I mean, sure, I'll come visit all the time, but still!"

"We understand. It would be too much to ask, especially after all you have already done for us, for a world not even yours. We are already indebted to you," Josh said, squeezing Lane's shoulder.

Lane sighed, relieved.

"LANE!"

Lane whirled around and saw all her friends running out to meet her.

"Hey guys!" Lane grinned as they all hugged her. The fairies wrapped their arms around her neck. She hugged them back tightly. As she carefully placed the fairies on the ground, Kinzie approached, giving her a big hug.

"Um … I hate to rain on the party, but Fayleen wants to see you. I think you need to go and see her before it is too late. She isn't doing well," Kinzie said, as she let her go. Lane nodded and started toward the castle.

Lane knocked on the door then pushed it open. As she slipped inside, tears threatened to spill over. There in front of her, lay Fayleen on her bed, leaning back on a small tower of pillows. She was lying on top of the covers in a simple white nightdress. She cracked her eyes and faintly smiled. That was all it took. Lane sniffed as the tears ran down her dirty cheeks. Fayleen stretched out her arms and beckoned her close. Lane padded over to the side of the bed and lifted herself up onto the edge to be closer. Fayleen wrapped her arms around her and let Lane cry into her shoulder. After sitting like this for a few minutes, Lane straightened up. Fayleen gently brushed her hand along Lane's tearstained cheek and smiled weakly.

"Why the tears?" Fayleen asked gently.

"Why? Do you really have to ask?" Lane tried not to start crying again.

Fayleen sighed. "Lane, everything must come to an end. I

have come to peace with that, as long as my kingdom is safe. My kingdom is safe, isn't it?"

"Yes. I faced my fears, and Witch Hazel will never hurt anyone again."

"Good," Fayleen nodded, relaxing her shoulders. "I just have one more question."

"I will answer as well as I can."

"When I am gone, and I am afraid that will be quite soon, I need someone to care of The Forest. I need someone to care for my people. I would like that person to be you."

Lane started to protest, but Fayleen continued, "But I know you want to go back home. I know you have your own life back through the tree. Which is why I want to ask you, who do you think would be a good choice?"

Lane was stunned by this question, but she knew exactly who to recommend.

Fayleen, sitting on her throne, placed her hands on Willow's shoulders. She smiled and stood up unsteadily, flanked by attendants. She placed her silver crown on Willow's head; and, while leaning on Josh's arm, she stepped away from her throne. And Willow took her place.

As Willow sat, Fayleen shakily spoke, "Now announcing Queen Willow Gale, the new protector, leader, wizard, and caretaker of The Forest."

From their place on the long wooden pews, all the witnesses launched themselves up and started cheering. Willow flushed with an overwhelming joy.

Afterward, Lane ran up and hugged her.

"I still can't believe you recommended me, of all elves, to Fayleen," Willow said, brushing her long, flowing, dark brown hair back behind her shoulders and it cascaded down her back to just below her waist. Lane had never seen it loose, and was surprised to see it was so long.

Lane shrugged. "She asked me who I thought would be the best choice. You are kind and caring; you are a natural born leader, a great friend, and you're awesome. I think you are going to do great." She gave her another loose hug.

"Well, thank you-" Willow stopped when she saw everyone running toward Fayleen. "Oh no." Willow and Lane took off running, both tripping over their long gowns. They started pushing through the crowd. Lane and Willow stopped cold. Josh and another young elf lifted Fayleen onto a stretcher, and the elves holding it hurried off, Willow right behind them. Lane tried to get to Josh through the crowd, the hum of the people loud in her ears. When she finally reached him, the look in his eyes told her it wasn't good.

"What happened?" she asked.

"She collapsed. Luckily, Luke and I caught her, but it's not looking good. We should go check on her. C'mon." Josh wrapped his arm around her shoulders and they hurried out of the hall.

Once they reached the room, Lane stood next to Josh and Willow as they all circled around Fayleen's bed. Fayleen's eyes fluttered open. As people started to speak, she held up her hand for silence. "Please let me speak," she whispered. She opened her mouth to speak again but fell into a coughing fit. A few of her attendants hurried forward, placing pillows behind her back to support her.

When she regained her voice, she spoke softly, "I know I chose correctly," she said smiling at Willow.

"I know you are a wonderful teacher, and you have been training the best warriors I have ever seen." She lightly gripped Josh's hand.

As Fayleen spoke to each of them individually, they just couldn't stop the tears. When she finally got to Lane, she smiled. Lane sat on the edge of the bed once more, and Fayleen held her close. Lane didn't want to let go. Fayleen eased her out to an arm's distance and spoke weakly.

"I know this was not easy for you. We asked too much of you. We asked you to risk your life to save us. And you did. You faced your fears. You overcame every obstacle in your way. You are courageous. You are our hero."

Lane sniffled as the tears streamed down. She simply nodded and slid off the bed. She took her place beside Josh. When she looked back at the bed, she saw Fayleen smile, and then a bright light shone. She shielded her eyes until it finally dimmed. When she removed her hands, Fayleen was gone, and a small crystal on a twisted silver chain lay in her place. Lane stepped over to the bed and picked up the necklace. She turned to face Willow and clasped it around her neck.

"This belongs to you now." Lane smiled, a single tear slipping down her face.

"Thank you," Willow whispered, hugging her.

11

GOODBYES AND GRANDPARENTS

LANE TURNED AROUND TO FACE HER FRIENDS. SHE was dressed in the clothes she had arrived in, but had an extra pair from the castle to use when she visited. Thanks to Willow, Lane had all her original things and more. Her camera and her mom's diary were safely tucked away in her jacket pocket, and her hair was back up in a pony-tail. Her crystal and leather necklace hung around her neck, hidden well under her t-shirt, and her silver-handled daggers were concealed by her jacket. She was ready to go home.

"Well, goodbye everybody," she said, smiling. The fairies

and dwarves each gave her a hug, and the fairies held on so tightly that Lea and Quinn had to practically pull them off. Then it was their turn to say goodbye.

"I'll bring you those pictures, I promise. I'll go get them developed," Lane promised Lea.

"Developed?" Quinn asked.

"I don't have time to explain, but Lea can tell you." Lane smiled at the young boy.

"Oh, ok. Well, I guess I will see you whenever you come back. I hope you come soon." Quinn said.

"Don't worry," Lane smiled, "I will. Fist bump," Lane said, sticking out her fist.

Quinn just looked at her, confused. "What are you doing?"

"Oh, um, it's something we do back in my world. You guys taught me lots of stuff, so let me teach you something. You just, make a fist, and tap in on mine, like this." Lane demonstrated.

"Awesome!" Quinn said, using one of the many words Lane had taught them. "Did I use that right?"

Lane laughed. "Yup!"

"Cool!" Quinn tried again.

Lea pulled him aside. "Don't get him started. We will never get him stopped." She rolled her eyes, but smiled.

"That's okay. Well, I guess I will see you guys when I get back." Lane hugged them again, and they went down the hill to the rest of the group. Josh was the only one left.

He sauntered over. "Hey. Willow wanted to be here, but she had to stay back at the castle. She said to tell you bye. So, 'Bye'," Josh said in a high-pitched, girly voice.

Lane laughed. "I don't think that imitation was very realistic, but it was a good try."

"Well, now that I got Willow's goodbye out of the way, I wanted to give you mine. Instead of mushy goodbyes and tears, I thought I would just give you this." Josh pulled a small package out of his pocket. Lane smiled as she unwrapped it, then gasped. Laying there, bundled in the cloth, was a small silver link bracelet with a small crystal hanging from it.

"Oh, Josh," Lane breathed. "I love it!"

"I saw the necklace that Fayleen gave you, but since you lost it … well, you have this instead."

"Thank you," Lane whispered, still staring at the gem. She was fascinated by its flawless identicality to her necklace.

"You're welcome."

She looked up at him and smiled.

"I probably should go," Lane said, glancing back at The Tree.

"Well, I guess I will see you when you come back."

"Yeah, I guess so," Lane said.

After a few awkward seconds, Josh pulled her in a hug. "Goodbye, Lane."

"Bye." Lane watched as Josh walked down the hill. She turned back to The Tree and smiled as she looked at the intertwining trunks, the deep green leaves, the gnarled roots … Lane took a deep breath, and stepped through.

Lane stepped out on the other side, and looked around. She was amazed by how different it was from The Forest. While it was spring in The Forest, it was autumn here, and Lane pulled her jacket a little tighter around her and shivered. Even for warm Tennessee, it was a little chilly. But that was the least of her worries.

She started to run toward the house reveling in the sound of leaves crunching beneath her feet. When she got to the edge of the woods, she smiled as she stepped from brown and grey woods to the green grass. She saw the farmhouse about a hundred and fifty yards ahead and took off running.

As Davy ran up to greet her, Lane knelt and buried her face in his chocolate hair as she hugged him.

"It's good to see you too, boy," she said scratching him behind his ear. "Where's Grandpa and Grandma, huh?"

The fact that the dog didn't answer was a sign that she wasn't in The Forest anymore. She ran up the stairs to the porch and slipped in the house. She looked over at the calendar on the wall. It still said September.

September?

Lane was confused by how that could be possible. She had been in The Forest for almost a month! Then she remembered what Fayleen had told her about the time spell on the tree. Just the thought of Fayleen was enough to bring tears to her eyes. She shook her head and went on a hunt to find her grandparents.

"Grandpa? Grandma?"

"In here, honey!" came Grandpa's voice from the kitchen.

Lane pulled off her cowboy boots by the door and padded over to the kitchen. Grandpa sat in a chair he had pulled from the dining room, and Grandma was pulling cookies from the oven. They obviously had been deep in conversation but dropped it when Lane walked in.

They are going to find out eventually about the nightmares and flashbacks. I may as well tell them now.

"Um, I need to tell you something."

That stopped both of them.

"What's wrong, honey?" Grandma asked, concerned.

"I um ..." Lane tried to stay calm. "I have been having

these nightmares. About the attack. And flashbacks too. I have worked through them as much as I can on my own but-"

"Lane! Honey, why didn't you tell us?"

"I didn't want you to worry."

"Lane, we love you. We want to help you in any way we can. We are always going to be here for you." Grandma promised as she hurried across the room, wiping her hands on her apron. She and Grandpa both hugged her.

"I had thought there was something wrong, but I had no idea," Grandma said. "I should have looked into it more. I should have done something-"

"Grandma, there was no way you could have known. Don't get upset."

"Why don't we go in the living room and have a nice long talk," Grandpa suggested gently.

12

HOME IS WHERE THE HEART IS

LANE SAT ON THE NEW, OLIVE GREEN ROCKING chair Grandpa had made for her, and she rocked back and forth, relaxing contentedly.

Davy lifted his big, brown eyes to her and whined.

"Sorry boy, am I neglecting on my petting duties?" Lane chuckled.

He laid his head on her leg, and grunted as she rubbed behind his ear. He only had a few seconds of calmness before spotting a squirrel, and, of course, off he went to chase it. Lane grinned as she saw him bounce around the yard wagging his tail. After losing hope of catching it, back he came.

"Oh no," she muttered. Her eyes widened. "No! Davy, NO!"

He leaped into her lap.

"OOMPH! Davy, you are definitely not a chihuahua." She tried to push him off, but he just sprawled out on his back and looked at her with his tongue hanging out of his mouth. His eyes danced. I think he's laughing at me.

"You lazy mutt!" Lane laughed, pushing at him.

"I know that's right," Grandpa chuckled, coming through the screen door.

"Hey, Grandpa."

"Hey girly. Um ... can I ask you a question?"

"Sure. That's how we get the answers." Lane smiled, using one of his own lines.

"Did you find what your mama loved so much? In the woods?"

Lane thought for a moment. "I think so."

"What was it?"

Lane smiled as she fiddled with the crystal on her silver bracelet.

"An adventure in The Forest."

THE END ... OF THE FIRST OF MANY ADVENTURES

Basic Character Index:

Alaina (Lane) Noel Jackson: Human, waist-length, bleach-blonde hair, blue eyes, round face, tall, pretty, lightly tanned skin, strong

Coral: Mermaid, peach tail with pearls and silver strands adorning it, sun bleached hair, ocean blue eyes, deeply tanned skin, beautiful

Fayleen Crystal: Wizard, long white hair, usually braided with silver strands weaved in, a silver crown with delicate, white gold flowers, detailed silver leaves, and small crystals adorning it. Warm gray eyes, pointed ears (as she was once an elf), pale skin, weak

Jack: Dwarf, bushy brown beard, burly, brown eyes, brown hair, four ft. tall, twin to John, the only difference being the color of their shirt. Red shirt

John: Dwarf, long, bushy, brown beard, burly, brown eyes, brown hair, four ft. tall, twin to Jack, the only difference being the color of their shirt. Blue shirt

Josh Clearbrook: Elf, brown hair, green eyes, very tall, pointed ears, strong, tan skin

July (Jules) Kymn: Fairy, gold hair, sky blue eyes, white cloud-like wings, yellow jonquil-petal dress, barefoot, sun-kissed skin

Kinzie Rayne: Elf, long brown hair, olive green eyes, tall, pointed ears, fair skin

Lea Roan: Elf, shoulder-length brown hair, pale green eyes, tall, pointed ears, lightly tanned skin

Oakley Kymn: Mop of shaggy brown hair, brown cow eyes, darkly tanned skin, light brown wings that have a wood-grain design on them, a shirt of sewn together oak leaves, leather calf-length pants, acorn-top hat, barefoot

Omah: Indian, long silver hair that falls to just above his shoulders, ice blue eyes, no shirt, tanned leather pants, leather moccasins, deeply tanned skin, white wolf pelt over his shoulders, strong

Quinn Fischer: Elf, short brown hair, dancing bright green eyes, tall, pointed ears, lightly tanned skin

Rose (Rosie) Kymn: Fairy, bright red and pink hair, delicate, pale yellow wings, sparkling green eyes, rose petal dress, rose leaves folded and sewn into shoes, fair white skin

Willow Gale: Elf, long brown hair braided tightly, soothing green eyes, tall, pointed ears, strong

Witch Hazel Black: Witch, long, glossy, raven hair, extremely pale skin, very thin, long black nails, eyes change between dark brown (near black) and a swirling red/orange, bewitchingly beautiful

Basic Creatures of Magic:

Wizards:
Wizards are elves that have been gifted with magic. It is rare, but when it happens, the wizard is extremely powerful. But not without control. They must train, and discover the best way to use their gift. Humans can train themselves to control magic, but again, it happens very rarely

Witches:
Witches are wizards that have chosen to use their gift for evil instead of good. Can be extremely manipulative

Conflagros:
Evil male wizards that have chosen to use their gift for evil instead of good. Can be extremely manipulative and powerful

Elves:
The most common race. But they have a few racial traits, as many of the creatures you will get to know will. They all have dark brown hair and green eyes (though shade of both may vary), and they are all tall and have pointed ears. All protectors of The Forest, and all the staff at the Crystal Castle wear similar clothes. They all wear brown bottoms, green tops, and brown shoes. They are usually friendly people, but they are

very protective, and can be fierce. Elves usually live in either Fayleen Forest, or The Elven Village. Many young teens come to the Crystal Castle for training

Dwarves:

A rather uncommon race, but not entirely rare. They are short. An average dwarf is about four feet tall, which makes people often mistake them for gnomes. They all have long beards (The men), or long hair (the women). They take pride in it, as they are very prideful creatures, and a dwarf's age and wisdom is determined by the length of their beard or hair. They are not all that bright, but what they lack in brains, they make up for in strength and skilled craftsmanship. They live in an area called Molton Mountain mines, which is a combination of three high peaked mountains just beyond the Oaken Forest

Fairies:

Surprisingly, this race is very common. As for their racial traits, their last name is determined by which village these fairies call home. And the second racial trait is size. All fairies are under a foot tall at full adult. They weigh about a pound. The most common, and the largest, village is called the Kymn Village. It is inside the Forest Of Fayleen, which makes it the safest of the villages

Gnomes:

These tricky little creatures are very smart, and very, very quick. This helps them in one enormous way. Theft. They are thieving little people that love to steal jewelry, coins, well, really anything they can get their hands on. They will also twist words and be very vague for their own advantage. Never accept one of their "promises". They are also quite short, much like dwarves.

Mermaids:

These mysterious creatures only appear once every few centuries, making them extremely rare. The only one we know of is Coral, who was appointed queen of the rivers by Wizard Fayleen Crystal. They are very kind, peaceful creatures

Dragons:

Large amphibian creatures with huge wings and a long tail and a gift. Color when born decides their gift. The most common are blue (ice/water) red (fire/transformation) black (fire/invisibility) and green (nature and healing). There are many more uncommon and rare colors. But color and gift have nothing to with the way they choose to use it. Some work for good, (being ridden, helping on farms, protection, etc.) but others work for evil (destroying villages, consuming innocent people and creatures, working for Witches and Conflagros, etc.).

About the Author

Lorryn is a homeschooled high school student inspired by her dreams, her father's stories, and constant reading to create her own fantastical worlds, creatures, and thrilling tales. She loves children and their adorable stories that give her hope and the belief that anything is possible as long as you keep dreaming. She wants to give them the same hope, and inspire them to write their own stories.

CPSIA information can be obtained
at www.ICGtesting.com
Printed in the USA
BVHW03s2259290618
520506BV00001B/120/P